CARNIVAL OF SLEEP

Ribitch

CARNIVAL OF SLEEP

Ribitch

OYSTER
MOON
PRESS
BERKELEY, CALIFORNIA

Carnival of Sleep
by Ribitch

Cover and interior illustrations
by the author.

ISBN: 978-0-578-08422-0

Previously Published:

A Dinner in the Hall of Ice
Somnambulist #1: Mytographic Press 1984
Third Morning/Nefftania
Opposite Shore Studios 1999
Morsels/Politicians of the Depraved/Mostainbo
The Somnambulist Footprints: Oyster Moon Press 2008
Delta Blues/Visions of Love on a Violent Sea
Hydrolith: Oyster Moon Press 2010

Special acknowlegment to Eric Bragg and Chuck Fahrenbach
for all their editorial help and advice.

Additional copies of this book can be ordered from LuLu:
http://www.lulu.com

Oyster Moon Press is a non-profit surrealist publishing
co-op that originated in Berkeley, CA.

CONTENTS

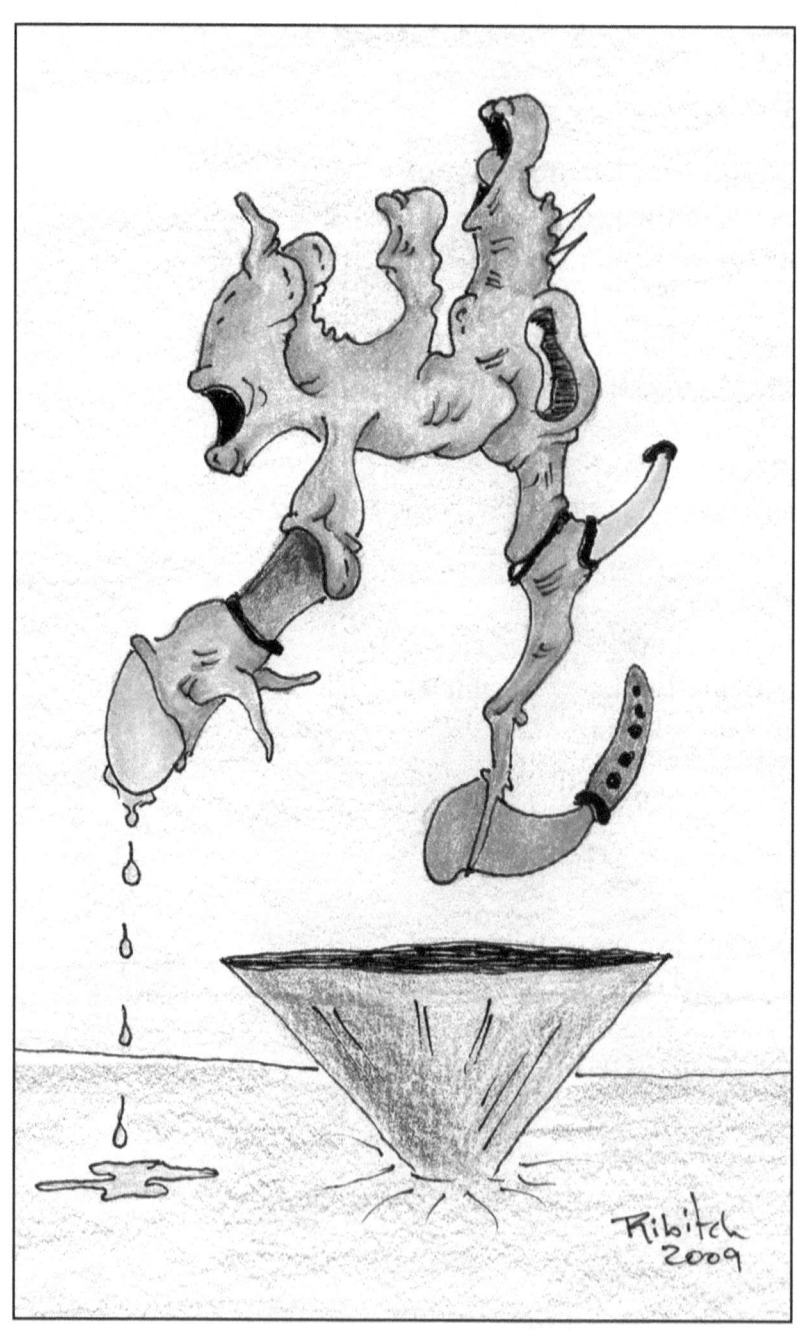

A DINNER IN THE HALL OF ICE

On the night of the darkest, when the moon has shown its full face clothed in black, a table is set, edged in ruby and crowned in pearl. For each of the guests is laid out a pair of serving gloves made of the finest filigree of fog. The gloves reflect the amber hues of the circular toasting candle upon which the somnambulist's shadows shall pass. On the third hour of meditative reflection a wine is served. The wine, served by the hands of Coltamine who is in the hundredth year of solstice to the moon, is thick and warm as blood. The first toast is made to the "Harvest of Planets," upon which dreams collide. The shadows of the somnambulists pass in reverent repose through the toasting candle.

The first course is brought in upon the back of an anteater, who balances delicately a crystal platter draped in velvety steam. The nearest somnambulist lifts the thin blanket of steam, places a thin veneer of the steam across its shoulder and sings the "Litany of the Silent Frost." The delicate wings of pearl acanthus glazed in luminous sauce of the jonquil are placed in rune engraved receptacles and passed through a flame with each bite in order to bake each individual spoonful.

The second course, being lighter than air, is served in clear glass globes carried in the mouths of musicological air fish, which consistently hum a microtonal dialogue. Each of the guests will insert a silver straw into the globes and draw forth through their nose, the vaporous and sensuous substance. The first of the somnambulists to burst forth into uncontrollable laughter stands and makes a toast to the presence of humor, and the shadows again pass through the toasting candle.

The third course, resembling multi-colored sand, is brought forth by dragonflies grain by grain and placed upon the lips of the guests, who exchange them with one another through a kiss. This delicacy of labial melting of the grains of osculation is savored slowly with meditative repose.

The fourth course, brought forth flaming like miniature suns placed upon soft petals of archidaceous blossoms of an anemone, is savored in the rich texture that comes with the colors of the dawn. Each tendril filled with succulent warm fluid is drawn forth with light sucking motions.

The fifth course, being invisible to the waking eye, but issuing the fragrant perfume of orange and spice with the delicate scent of morning wind, is eaten by the shadows of the somnambulists. They then transfer its vitality to the waiting tongues of the somnambulists.

The sixth course, a very large fungus of multiple forms and colors, is transposed upon the table by holographic means and is tasted by the guests at their leisure and capacity to indulge in illusion.

The seventh and final course, brought in by an array of exotic unheard of forms of zoology, is placed in front of each guest upon a velvet napkin. The color and brilliance of this final delicacy is of ruby. It is spoon fed to the guests by invisible servitors. The taste of almond with a hint of Madagascar mint is present.

A final toast is made to the endearing luminescence of the moon as a thin mist gathers about the feet of the guests. The shadows pass for the last time through the toasting candle, followed by the somnambulists leaving Coltamine, who is in the hundredth year of solstice to the moon.

THE SEVERED BLADE OF MEMORY

I tried to step out of my wombat suit, the one with silver and tweed lining, when I was accosted by the wall. The wall was a fragrant green of a rain forest. There was a bus toilet in the corner. Three men dressed in blue knit suits played pinball with the clock. A nun sang songs and had violent tears made of rock. A glass point broke off in my hand. I cried, and my tears hung from the ceiling. "What dreams count the sighing blue of my breath flying?" I asked the crystal tears that hung from the ceiling like blue domes. I walked across the room, hoping it would disappear. The windows were painted on. The paint was still wet. "I know you all," I said, pointing to an imitation Van Gogh that hung on the wall where my face used to be. The Starry Night beckoned me and I turned my head with embarrassment.

There was a bleeding wrist that played with the dog on the floor. It was an open wound that spoke like the sky. My mouth was dry. My eye folded itself like a paper airplane. There was a horse sitting on the sofa. He addressed me with a laugh, "Did you know the blank stares of the blind?" He winked at me with his toothy smile. "There is a pontiff glade of rose blood to soften the axe of dreaming eagles."

"I spoke of you once," I replied.

"In death you walked with me, wearing my saddle," he spoke with his lips quivering.

"And...?" I muttered.

"Ah..." he replied, lifting his muzzle and letting his tongue hang in the air. I reached out to him with my hands swollen, and they were bleeding. There was a mountain of dung with a smile. The horse placed himself inside a silver cage. "You have dreamt it a thousand times and you have fondled the moments with your eyes held blank. Your flowers grow from pots of ash; they are not what they seem, why don't you go to the mirror and look?"

I walked to the dresser mirror and peered long into its reflection. I wasn't content with the pictures of past roses and my hand seemed to travel onward, deep inside the mouth of the mirror. I greedily followed my hand, searching beyond the glass and beyond my groping fingers. The Horse called out, "If you find it, let your eyes explore it and don't let your hunger stampede your search for what resembles the truth."

9

I turned to answer but the mirror was now gone and what lay before me pulled at my eyelids. There was no place for a station, but people lined up in twos, waiting for a bus, while a small boy moved in and out of the line. "Pillows, newspapers, cigarettes, suicide notes," he called out. The bus was obviously late. Sweat formed on the brows of the waiting passengers, their fingers twitched nervously. I took my place in line and purchased a pillow and newspaper from the boy.

When the bus arrived, I felt a sigh of relief such as felt when someone is expecting a great turn of events. The scuffling of moving feet grew to a roar in my ears. I swallowed hard and gathered my breath. I boarded the bus. The driver's head wore a death mask. He grinned at me as I passed him. All the passengers sat silently staring ahead, hands in their laps. There was a nervous quiver about their manner and I could feel the vibration of the air. It shook me till I trembled all over. I felt the bus jerk forward, leaving behind a place I've never been. The bus had an ominous silence about it. My tongue was dry. There was the smell of urine connecting everybody's feet. I glanced about, letting my eyes rest on the neck of the passenger in front of me. I sat there gathering all the faces of former lifetimes into my memory.

There was a clown sitting next to me. His costume was soaked in blood. "There are willows of death on this bus," he said, as he adjusted his enormous bow tie and looked dead ahead.

"Do you have the time?" I asked.

"Oh, I have all the time in the world," he replied.

"No, the time of day, what hour is it," I asked.

"It's ever since and never again," he said. He turned his face toward me and smiled. His teeth were rotten and yellowed, his breath was vile.

"I have seen these faces before," I said while glancing around the bus.

"That is a possibility that rings from the hunger of your youth," said the clown. He removed his hand and placed it in mine. "What will it take to clutch your heart, and will it squeeze a millennium of uttering? I myself have been here a century, and even then my disguise is only the picture of a presumed reality."

"You are a clown?" I asked.

"You are a clown," he said. There was a deafening silence and the hand turned into a rose. I turned to look at the clown for some explanation of the occurring event, but he had become a rose bush. "The bars on your cell are made of glass; it is an illusion that taints your eyes; if you only let go of reason and logic, you will then see a fine bird of colored feathers."

I groped at the bush, frantically bloodying my fingers, but the bush laughed. It laughed and laughed and my fingers bled. Looking to the rest of the bus, I discovered that all the passengers had turned into rose bushes. They were all laughing. The laughter grew in my ears till it burst in my head. It was only the driver and me now. I sat back in my seat, breathing hard and the laughter turned around in my head. The driver's death mask covered my eyes. What could I tell from my dreams, the great plays and fecal images that fall upon my mind? "It is an illusion," I thought. I played with my thoughts and stripped the magnetic blue grace with a transfusion of words. There had been a spell spoken in unknown tongues and images. A fly crested itself backward and licked the want from my eyelids. The bus seemed familiar to the unknown lands and treaded in the footsteps of vagrant beasts. I sat in the seat and waited, watching the sands bleed into the horizon. In my ears I heard a vibrant voice of a poet singing:

> *"Wait for the long masters*
> *who wield their blood stained tears*
> *as birds contracting the lover's hips*
> *and the oval solitude of fragrant musk,*
> *the opalescent mask speaks in tongues*
> *to the wind that romances the blackened flowers*
> *that drinks the watery bliss of fiery monoliths.*
> *The dungeon of ants smells the rage of crystal factories*
> *urge the cracked mill grinder's wheel,*
> *into prophecies of untold valor."*

The bus hinged itself forward like a giant centipede, rocking along hungrily at the peak of frustration. I felt heaviness and slept. I seemed to sleep forever, as if in a glass booth.

I dreamed of fish with the beaks of birds. They were walking on the land, carrying suit cases and pillows. I tried to stop one, and it bit off my arm. As an armless man, I felt like a fool. One of the beaked fish approached, drooling a white viscous-like filth down my chest and it fevered itself upon me. I next dreamed of an old lady. She stood on a wax

11

box and held needles in-between her fingers. When she tried to speak, soap bubbles came from her eyes as tears. She turned into a rabbit and was slaughtered. The rabbit's spilt entrails formed the words, "The black night eats the gallant dust of fingers." My final dream was a black void. I floated in the nothingness of space. My tongue was swollen and stuck in my throat. I felt breathless. My lungs seized up in my chest, and I awoke.

The driver had his hands at my neck in a grip of steel. My eyes were fixed on his, and there was a flame in them. "It is time to leave," he said. A demonic grin creased his face.

"What?" I cried out, shaking the sleep from my head.

"The end of the line," he replied. "You may disembark now and play with your destiny. You may go and linger with your dreams or nightmares, whatever you choose." His sardonic grin bit into me, and I felt the pain of his eyes' grip. "Remember to take your reason with you, you may have the opportunity to bathe in its falseness."

Once off the bus, I felt the sun's heat, baking the hard earth beneath my feet. The bus left me standing. I watched it fade in its dust and wondered at the curious content. I then stood there alone, fingering the dust of miles away thinking of romantic gestures and the symbols of my dreams. The sands licked at my feet and sang tunes in my ears. An elephant walked past me carrying the headless fortunes and gold rings of the ghosts of the kings of the desert. The road that stretched out before me was made of postage stamps and complained of bad dreams. I felt a lump of vomit in my throat. There was a woman standing off to my right. She had roses growing from her eyelids, and she held her entrails in her hand. She had decapitated my words before they reached my mouth, and she sewed them into a silk pouch stained with blood. She stood frozen like a ghost, her lips moving almost indistinctly, words I could barely hear. "The olive branch breeched your love like the syllables of a long word turned inside out," she said. "There are moments of dream that touch moments of reality."

"Let me…," I muttered, trying to get the words from my mouth.

"No," she replied. "There is no need and no way. My insides secrete my outsides, and that's lost in the vibrant sun eating at what were my eyes. If you must, then cut off my arms and let them be taken by crows. Allow yourself to be turned inside out. Rip the buttons off your eyes, swallow your brains and cry the blood tears of ancient times."

"I don't understand," I said. "I just don't get it."

"Oh, you know." She said. "You've looked before at your scant insanity, but you have always quickly glanced away."

"That's not true," I replied.

"Yes it is, and your blood history can prove it," her eyes revealed a knowledge as old as time.

"What do you know of my blood history?' I asked.

"As much as the mirrors of your heart," she replied. "Look," she demanded, producing a mirror from her skirt. "Look at yourself, a contained history book of infamy, of flame, of death and disgust. Look at them and yourself, and feel the heat of fire." She let the mirrors loose and they flittered in the air like fireflies.

I looked at the wandering mirrors, dancing under the moon, their cold glances seeming awkward. I was an infant. I was a child. I was an adolescent looking for meaning. I was an adult swooned in the collar of tragedy. The hypothesis of my existence exploded in a thousand dreams. The carrousel spun, with me dizzy in the eye of a hurricane. Blood came to my mouth so I could not speak.

"Look!" she screamed. "Look at yourself; you're a fool in the desert of tasteless morgues. The swollen feet of dancers are the bricks to build your house." I tried to close my eyes, but they were pried open with sticks. I tried to shout, but my mouth was sewn shut with golden threads. I tried not to hear, but my ears had blaring trumpets. "You're an ass," her voice quivered in the night air. "I shall cut your memory with scissors and put each half in a separate box, and you shall stand on them for all eternity."

The air was dry. The bone parched dryness of the air is all I could feel. She stood there with her breast open. The past was a needle in the air. "Why don't you give me what's mine?" I said. "All that I ever was belongs to me."

"You can stand before the world," she said, "with a naked quiver, cold and alone on the beach of nothing. Your whole life is raining before you. It even makes holes at your feet. There are books left open and they can see you through the pages, and you claim it is yours, like you forgot what it was all about. Even as your father stood outside your window exposing the masturbation that secreted from your desire, you still claim it all as your own. Look again into the closet where you keep your hidden secrets. There are bleachers set up and they are full of clapping people."

I closed my eyes, and when I opened them, there was a crowd of people sitting in bleachers. I was on some sort of parade ground; the crowd was laughing. The laughter grew louder and louder till I couldn't stand the sound. Suddenly it stopped. Silence! I could feel the strange eyes deflesh me, peeling me like an orange. A man dressed for some sort of ceremony approached. He wore a top hat and tails, with a carnation in the lapel. His medals gleamed in the sunlight. I stood very still, in a pose of complete attention. He stopped right in front of me, his thick mustache kissing the sky. A second man came up beside the first, carrying a highly decorated box. He opened it. The box contained a single calling card. The first man removed the card and placed it into my hands. He then kissed me on both cheeks. Both men turned and walked away. I stood there in the silence, with the crowd intently staring. I felt I had been bestowed a great and noble honor. I turned the card over in my fingers, feeling the weight of it. I put it up to my face and read. There in gold script it read, "GUILLOTINE."

Swisssssh! Thud! Ring! This was the sound of the blade hitting a chopping block. The crowd again began to laugh. It was a hard, side-splitting laughter, shaking the crowd in the bleachers. A loud woman's scream came from behind me. I turned. The laughter continued. There stood tall the fallen guillotine, the blade gleaming in the light. The screaming woman stood beside it with her hands held to her face. "They have beheaded him!" she cried. The guillotine stood empty. More laughter! It was a head-splitting laughter that rang in my skull. "They have beheaded him!" she cried out again. "For the sake of entertainment, they have committed an execution. Their orgasm is complete."

I approached to console her. "Look," I pointed out. "The guillotine stands empty."

"Only dreams that occur at the precise hour of midnight remain empty." She reached into the basket and removed a grapefruit, which she placed on the block. She pulled a knife from her blouse and raised it high in the air. As the knife came down, splitting the grapefruit, she swore into my face. "But ours, tonight, are full of the bestial execution of millions, who laid their heads before this quivering blade." She tapped the wooden frame of the guillotine with her fingers. "This wood is not so old as to not drop the blade a few more times. My head, your head, who knows, but when it does the clang shall be heard in a thousand dreams that awaken the dreamer from a restless sleep."

The crowd started to whisper. It was a low sinister whispering. "Glass eye, dog tooth, angel throat, flower wilt, ring coat, deep hole, sleep tight, good night, robbers, tigers, madness, foam nose, nothing, nothing, nothing."

"We must leave here," I said.

"Here, step into this telephone booth," she urged. The phone began to ring. "Answer it, it's for you."

I answered it. A voice spoke to me, crackling over the receiver: "Eat an umbrella." (CLICK!) I stood there motionless while the woman began to sneer at me. Her teeth were long and pointed. Her finger nails were sharpened like razors. They dug into my flesh. The glass booth shattered. It exploded around my ears. A thousand voices were speaking. Sharp severing glass fell. Thousands of people were laughing. Then nothing! There was no woman with sharpened teeth, no crowd bellowing laughing thunder, no guillotine, nothing. No ground existed under my feet, nothing. No sky over my head, nothing. Nothing but a soft white cotton nothing. I was not standing, not sitting, not laying down, nothing but white-cotton nothing.

Then as if from the back of my mind, a mere thought of my own was caught somewhere between my brain and my mouth, it was memory. Memory is an open face of jeweled tomorrows. Then there was more white cotton nothing, a nothing that stuffed itself up my asshole, forcing its way into me.

I felt a desire to push, and I did so. I felt a gasp of air. Push! Air! Push! Air! The cotton separated. I was blinded by light, bright and fixated. Air! Light! My ears exploded by the sound of voices, strange and unheard of. Slap! Pain! Like the intentions of sweet melodies, something was freeing. Voices garbled in the early morning haze. A cold harsh light blinded me. I exited into a fashionable room. Green clad giants loomed about me. They moved swiftly, talking amongst themselves. I make out the words: "Congratulations it's a boy." There was a swift movement of the green giants. I peered around me, past the light and there behind the green giants, standing tall and erect: THE GUILLOTINE!

15

THE DEAD GIRL ON A TRAIN

Her eyes were bright and terrible

Her mouth caught in a haunting grin

She stared at the passing countryside

As the train made its way

Through snow-covered fields

The resting harvests of white

The slow rumble of the wheels

Made my ears hurt in their drone

I watched her head bob

As if she were a toy with an eternal nod

Her blond curls falling short of her neck

Were eerie ringlets of spider's webs

She turned slowly to face me

Her eyes were bright and terrible

Her mouth caught in a haunting grin

The round mouth opened and mouthed silence

That made my hair move as in a wind

She brought up her pale, fat little hand

In a gesture of beckoning

I reached to touch but found only air

And scribbles upon the frosted window pane

A picture of her youthful face

Her eyes were bright and terrible

Her mouth caught in a haunting grin

AMONGST THE SPIDER WEBS, JEWELS ABOUT YOUR NECK

(For Marie Toyen)

We have met at some time
amongst the shadows of
a hallway interlaced
with the osculation of the breezes.
The mirrors with their silver jackets
and the secret breathing
found in the waters of the Amazon.
The fish with harrowing cloaks of sequins.
The lion whose mane
is the brush of my cheek.
This hallway in which I speak
is laced with spiders' webs crossed with
the flavor of a silk purse.
What was it hidden beneath my eyelids,
covered with a thin layer of wax?
The whispers of the night
with its mood tied to my sleeve.
We have met at some time.
The shadows will never part
because no scissors can unbind them.

A DANCE WITH DEATH

The remedial flash of my squandered wanderings are as if they lifted my somnambulant past. Death is a rose that floats before the eyes quilted and crazy. The gray of hope fled past the sea, where onlookers search their stockings for pubescent wanderers. Their nails are filed down, clean and even. Death for them is the gray whale of their honor. Honor for them the stolen clocks that keep their youth, and death is that rose of plain heaven. That rose that wilts in the sand like my eyes. My heart reaches out to touch the silk strands of faces that hover near me. I call out to death, "Rose, tender sheath of death, thin sheet of paper burning. My eyes can't conceal for a moment the dark hand that slips past my throat."

Death stands there like a dark horse in the wind, sober with its tail tied to its sex. Sabers clean through its middle. The rose of plankton, I know you now. Over and over, it is the degree of your burning touch. Rose, your death is speaking to me in open palms. That moment I await that shall shake the fine dust of Hermes. His fingers are yellow, caked and worn of their duty. No longer a messenger to the gods, but he is unduly the half-promises of a clip in time. Death, you half-tied your knot. You have taken me under your wings of lead and taken me fresh into the springs of life. My voice quivers the salt of time. Kept in a bottle and refreshed like the soil that caresses my feet.

My voice like you raised, wilts under the hot beating sun. It recoils in the plankton of frost that holds me erect. What noble prices you ask? My flesh or spirit? My years upon years? Rose of red flesh, I can at last see your face. It resembles mine, only in the slightest degree. As I pass by the graveyard of my nimble soul, there amongst the grove of willows stands white marble, marking the edge of time. Time that endurable beast that speaks with no tongue. Time that placid marking in my chest. Past, present and future all kept in the same vessel. They cannot be drunk by me. No! I refuse to partake of its disgusting ordure.

Wings, if I had for a moment wings, I would take flight into the blackness of space, chasing innumerable white felons of crazy belief. In addition, wings I have, for my flight is not complete without the fire of the sun in my heart. Death, sweet luscious melody is the fragrance of musk. I chase you to the doors of perception. I follow you in seeking lost truths that I may never find. Death is the alibi of disfigured saints. I find moments of need to find myself in the least bit of preparedness. My bags have been packed and unpacked. My level eye searches for a mere glance into the dark doorways of your chambers.

I believe that I have more to combat than the fangs of delicious desire. My heart pounds out on such drums. My feet feel the slightest movement of the earth where soil mingles with worms to seek my beating heart. To tell me untold secrets of the unfolding years will make me weep. I wait. I wait, wait for the gestures to awaken before me and to scream my eyelids from their youthful existence. I have become a spectator of my own life. Their metamorphous flower, decay, die and is reborn, suckling the wind with infant tears. I am and I will be as I have been. This I proclaim: that my lips, like silver vessels contain the speech of ancient Egyptian pharaohs, who in their dark sleep, touch me with their voices in the nocturnal quietude of endless flight. They sit at the end of my bed, counting the figures of my dreams.

Death, I know you well. You have become my brother a dozen times. I have placed you in the well and you have escaped me. We have played chess for the price of the night. It is of no matter, for you exist only as far as I permit. My reality can be as permanent as yours. We exist only to choose each other in the dance on the other side of the mirror. We and I use the we not as lightly as you might think, crossing in front of each other, eyeing each other like cats before battle. You know the curves of my thoughts, and I know yours, like my own set of teeth. There is a melody that begins to play. We dance under the moon, you and I. Death and the fool. Death is the slayer of dragons. We dance smiling. Our lips are curled back in defiance. The moon bears witness. The earth utters in awe. We dance the dance we have danced before. There beyond the shadows lies the sword with which I wish to slay you. There beyond your eyes lies your weapon to slay me. Moreover, we dance as the night yearns on.

As our lips part we kiss the others' cheek, for one is Judas to the other. Death, I unmask you, and you are my image of youth. Death, I proclaim your story is untrue. My sword clutched firmly in my hand, I run it through your heart. You only claim your true faith in justice as time tilts the other way and the chase is resumed, as we await the next dance.

THE LIMPID YOUTH

Sitting in a room of questionable lions' livers that hover above umbrellas waiting for open doors to secrete a thick blood. After the dawn, a little wafer of mouths follows in close pursuit. Sometimes manifested as an image, the pale frost that leans against the windows, extends itself without the bellows that fornicate rust and fools, and the frost that leans on the windows are animals' teeth. Does that surprise you?

I am persistent in my mingling with the fog-like hands that are really wolves' ears. Even the umbrella under my arm contracts the cold noses of constant perspiration yield a holocaust of flags and bran. Sending sandals of rice to fill the cracks full of sniffles so those blades of swamp fern break out in a rash of flame. A large sandwich of pillars assaults a bludgeon of aphrodisiac convulsions and tied it to the hot bed of its colossal magnet head. A small piece of Camembert cheese is in the shape of a volatile mouse.

Somewhere the bark of maidens is like the lisp in the voice of clouds after extracting its teeth. The secret cry of she-wolves harbors the vanity of ocelots. Ink spilt beneath a cabinet of scars, each droplet a shadow of an exposed spine. The swallowed sighs conclude at the end of the mass, a harpooned figure with twilight hungering after the exposed fingers. A dog is swallowing your tongue with incredible swiftness. With knives pressed to the shoulder, the wine of the evening caresses the blood of whispers and wears patent leather pumps to gorge on a woman's breast on a table of obtuse silence. With the incredible gasp of the dawning, an iron staple is removed from the fountainhead of your insane gestures. Does that surprise you?

UNMASKING THE PRIVATE
PLEASURES OF WOLVES

The moon fills my eyes full of eyeglasses
The shuttered heart
The wolves awake amongst the brambles
Shedding light where closets stare
A whisper of the hound
            My hand lifts my face
Above doorways, granite and sable
The fish are wreaths
A blossoming explosion
Heat, transparent like the leaves of smoke
Birds perched on the edge of my heart
            Transfixed
Breathing great gulps
Blue flesh, an otter of wealth
A wreath of blood
Soiled toward a beacon of voices
            Squinting in the wind
Staring past corn wallows
Silver springs and hot defiance
The shivering dawn
The fountains of blood hurtled
Where walls explode
Feet follow their shadows deep into cracks
            Of a milling voice
A voice of numbers that have no fingers
Watching for airs of pearl
The quickened breath
The fleeced hat of bridges
Following a nervous gas
Inciting a riot where wings know
            Their blood wedding
And toward dawn the day explodes
Fires of silk worms

The persistence of chance warning
Warming the flood of bones
Automobiles tired of breathing
Their hands flow with milk
Designs where cabinets filled with dust
Walk about shaking the monolith's explosion
Explosion, burst from the stomachs of chimera
The floating potable of resins
      Spark the rest of the denseness
The window of my apartment grows
Great hairy tortoises
Wanting to run in wells
Where fish sing slight praises
And motion of the heart
A trembling forecast
Disbursing fluids of spark
The tank of ingression
Molting amongst the ducks who seek death
Only to sing its whispers
That carry no tunes other then the voice of the cypress
My mind is filled with ospreys
My heart is filled with earthquakes
My tongue is filled with feathers
      Set on fire
Vestibule of sponsored delusions
A black bird lifting bloody wings to a boat of sighs
Thunder, my breath is a laser
The smoking wombat walks toward a hunger
Shaken with fingers thought of wire
Wallpaper with frozen tigers
Tears under knot holes
      Banners fretting
Suicide settled in the ashes
Voices longing on the rafters that grow
      With the hungry wind
Soft palatable sting burst from eyelids
Motion, the whispers dance of arachnids

Hallways full of opiate smells
The fish walk in their blisters
      Shaking their fists
Nervous, a bone bleached on seclusion
Hyper logical inflammation
The forest is full of cigarettes
Frenchmen in wine glasses
Attaché case full of birds
      And their bones of silk
Their whispers, moons in my eyes
A wolf calls out to the spree of his fellows
Wanting to rip a shirt that I inhabit
Explosions, the quivers, the ripples
The El Diablo, the monk
      The spear of their fishes
Tomorrow will display an accident among the leeches
Their frail flowers blooming in nuptial disguise
A disguise of death heads and fleas
Running forth where dust sings
      But has no voice
An acrid desert that burst flesh
Upon sands of ancient sandals
Whose own flesh distracts the lonely cries of egrets?
The smell of the room
A lion is playing solitaire with hunks of bone
The lens of a microscope is stealing youth
      On a banner of tongues
Clad with iron shackles
Stooping for fly envelopes
Flowers of passion
The rain revealing blood
      Man
      Wolf
      Vampire
Silence walks away with the sleeves of a coat
That speaks with silent gestures
Debating the fossil's fortune

The shadows of man with his bloody tentacle of sex
The shadows of a bird drenched in sand
Crying out, the night has been poisoned
The lips lying inert on a bed of clouds
Murdered through passion's grief
A sail of swans
       With wings made into hallways
The murdered stir in the explosions of life
The blood of the redheaded eye
The shaking sinister boot
The double face and double hand
A landscape of screams
The parable leaks a gas of breath
       Man
       Wolf
       Vampire
The sun waits for the moon to charge
When sense extends beyond the gallows
The rope transfixed an eye on an eye
The shadows of a bird
       Of a century
       Of the cracks in the porcelain sky
Forming words that have no shadows
Shadows whose only words hide from letters at large
The cable extends
The nervous parade of their feet dissolved
Rose lips of wine
Winter of clouds
Dreams of passion
The shadow's caprice complete in the waltz
       Of a century
       Of cracks in the porcelain sky
I see the wolves embark and follow the rain's footsteps
Through the corridors
       Of laughter's interpreter
Something staggers
It's a vase of faces

The wheel rolling, leaving imprints
Footprints of quackery
A revolver on a carrousel
The horse's haunch
      Man
      Wolf
      Vampire
The fetters are glued envelopes
Antelopes like wax dolls
Entertain the evening with spikes
Entertain the illusion of darkness
The spider's shadow
And a crystal iguana that lights up the night
Count me missing among the missing
Take all the mirrors and unfold their flags
Fortune is kissing fortune
On the mouth of chiliads
The fire has sought to tango
      Beneath the wreaths of blossom
The sky with its collage of soldiers
With their heads of dark tunnels
From which gargoyle birds bloody their feet
File through the shadow's shadow
The secret bondage
The laced hearts
The figures of marble
The voices full of red sound
      Man
      Wolf
      Vampire
Approximately a drawer full of dreamers
Mine I've seen pass through the shadows
Chased by headless villains
      Never
      Never
Count me missing among the missing
The angle of the room with strange music

The child floating above the doggerel corpora
Laughter beneath the bowels of the moon
Sublime like a cat's eye
The roost of flame
The day that is night's bark
The villain beneath the quicksand
Albumin of voices sunk deep into cloud's bed
Cockerel follows the clock's hands
Round to the sunken fountain
       Where a woman broods with insects
Beneath a swollen leg that hovers in the sky
Like a thousand birds
       And a ring of silence
The glass spine
Turning in the leafy forest of sponge
Exercising disbeliefs in an excursion
Mauve anime attacks something
       Wildly alluding
The voice of an eagle
Its wings of bat furious
Congealed midway on the fox's hunt
The sky setting beneath the horizon
Digging a trench that worms forgot
A moldy pathway of sudden violence
Digging a trench that worms forgot
Those hollow rooms, those hollow minds
The pervading encasement
Vessels that hang from the moon
Casting shadows over their shadows
Their dogs remain
Their dogs finished something tasteful
Mandible on the head of grasshoppers
Who weep with the blades of grass
       The same as they,
       The same as they
The same as the silhouettes that accuse the dawn
The silhouettes with fish heads

The silhouettes with as many arms as spiders
The silhouettes with stilettos
        Or voices transparent as acetate
Who stitch the moon to the floor of the room
With smokes or sleeves or certain smells
The alpine frost outside the locked chambers
The doors sealed from prophesy
Wildly distributed amongst the shadows
The bleating life
The heat of somnambulant afternoon
The hair of a woman who flames mist
The hair of a woman walking in the pocket
The hair of a woman waking beneath the clouds of day
The hair of a woman gone to lunch with sparrows
Fish nets sigh beneath her
Forgetting every afternoon to dance like locus
That sings with voices of lumber
The burning that makes the afternoon laughter
Somewhere in the sperm and shadow
Eyelids filled with the moon's moan
Running crush, lungs explode a whisper of silence
Louder then a tremble that resembles the night
Night with its dreams of frozen collars
Decked in the dawn with pearls
        Weeping with fountains
The shadow's shadow
Standing with egrets at the edge
        Of milky laughter
Whispering the red bricks of the sun
Taunting the daylight to receive darkness
Carrying it beyond the horizon's tunnel of darkness
Laying it with the feathers and filigree of smoke
That elude silence somewhere
        In the secret eyes of future fires.

MORSELS

"The Moon"

The years of pantomime, a mask or a judge, a whisper of a night that smells like lizard. A room filled with glass, the moon, the frozen stooped shoulders of a claw in an evening gown designing flesh. I disrobe the mantle over a precipice of impossible disfiguration and the laughter that moves about the room is clasping hands. The light, the moon, the womb, the period of darkness beneath the storm. Hair, bandoliers of breath, fingers twitching where the mountains crust scab splits, spilling a black blood across the skies' swollen chest. The years of porcelain, swelling in an immense throat, where voices trembling in a blade of monkey blood. Nothing quivers like the quiet solution. The earth barks back. The moon, the womb, an egg filled with grasshoppers ready to explode in a crystal shroud of forbidden whispers. The moon, the womb, and a face that lingers with the deep-breathing wells that haunt with the night's skin.

The room stumbles; the shank of my leg detaches itself from my body and promenades before me, hung in a handkerchief. I look at the woman, who looks into a dark mirror. Her feet are caught up in thorns; a wasp is hung on her thighs, her thighs that are wooden ships with sails of powder moth wings and perfume. A midget clings to her legs, grotesque and twisted; he is an image wearing a black robe that smells like cat. He looks like a cat, the soft fur running off his face, the slight tilt of his pointed ears. "Uranus, your moons," She said. "My clitoris is hanging from the stars. The blood is my lips separated with the horizon's soft pink legs. Uranus, savory juice of love! Uranus, the moons of your folded smile elude toward the rivers of infancy. My lips hunt the fox. My vagina is grass and the seed of the sun. The stars exclude the horizon that bleeds in my palms. Morning moistens its thighs on my eyes of locust and my tongue of burning oil."

My heart moved in a circle. The twitch of a song split through the night with its warnings of herons. The woman stepped within a circle, dragging the midget, who opened his wings. The night was full of blues and the sweet weeping alabaster of arms. The night of contagion in my legs stretched into glass harps. I found it hard to speak, but finally my vocal chords released themselves. "I came here because I heard you were a teller of fortunes," I said.

"The future is like the ringing of silent bells," she cried. "A heart in the sky, the moon, the moon. A feather floats as time. You came not for the fortuneteller's wheel, but for all time's sunsets. The past with the dead knocking for entrance into the present; the present is like a fool on the border of sanity and the future is an automobile run out of gas. Nothing shall return but the alchemist glass, and with it the letters of science shall be broken. You came not for the future, but for the moon."

"The moon?" I asked.

"The womb," she replied.

"The womb?" I asked.

"The frozen specters on this desert," she replied.

The midget looked up at me with his eyes a cold white. Hunger lingered within the shadows of his face. A carousel horse danced across his lips. He spoke! "Are you afraid of the night?"

Everything puzzled me. I looked around for something familiar. I spied an old hat and placed it on my head weeping. The woman lit a candle and formed a circle around it. "The moon," she said. "And the mirror reflecting Uranus, the gown's shadow and the mist. Swallow the night, swallow the night. We first walk through the doorways of a darkened tent. Pass through the dream. The tent waits."

"The Tent"

I entered the tent, which smelled of bread and sandalwood. The tent was entirely black except for silver patches, cut into various positions of the moon. The tent was entirely devoid of furniture and objects, except for a red cape which was illuminated by the moon patches. By curiosity or intuition, I was led to sit beside the red cape. There was a bowl of red fluid sitting upon the red cape, into which I gazed. The fluid shimmered as if it were crystal, as if it were a voice of fishes, as if the morning were samples and the light were seas of flesh.

I sat for what must have been several hours, the dark silence a gloved hand over the tent's mouth. My body felt heavy, as if it had been sprouted from enormous wings. My breathing was a rhythmic force of songs, like frogs, like coyotes, like spiders, like all the creatures that speak with the moon. The silence was soft but had sharp edges. Something stirred in the air like a brush with the breeze or the smoke of sensation. It felt like a salamander's storm or a winter full of smelts. The grey dawn with its arms dressed in lace; a face dressed in dreams; I heard a voice as sweet as salt. "Enter the moon of the first part, the golden diatessaron and the carousel of sleep." I fell into a deep slumber and dreamed.

"The Dream"

A wombat fell out of space, caressing in its arms a fog that was not truly clear and seemed to bleed across the floor. The eyeglass, a hole in the center of the earth; from it rose a smoke as sweet as the rushes. The seams split open throwing forth great spasms of shrill smoke. A white light was in the passage of the second darkness, the second swallow and the second hunger. The passage into the smoke smelled of fish with their arms wound around a secret voice, the voice of dry cracked leaves. I lead three faceless horses toward a pond of silver. Stalks of grain rise out in a display of wreaths. The tips of each bleed translucent ruby red. If the faceless horses separate, stairways are revealed. Stairways to where? The horses run past, splintering the air, but they are devoid of the light of space. Awakened from sleep, I wander amongst the debris of snails, wandering where the first step takes the second going. I desire the length of a wall or beyond the mixture of advantageous delusion.

"The Stairway"

The stairway did not go down or up, but at a horizontal illusion. That is to say perpendicular to the wind. I know that my legs are thrown back. Time does not exist in the parallel, only strange whistles and faint figures that parade through the misty hallways of ambiguities smile. The ambiguous stairway and the forgotten object are like an ostrich in the act of disappearance. The perspective of a well in mutation is far too deep. The stairway is like a voice caught in a tunnel, translucent and invisible, a raging forest of sensuous arms. Frogs cough bitterness in the roots of playful laughter. I enter the stairway entering me, following the dawn's hermaphrodite through the stairwells of hallucination, through my eyes of moon thighs.

My lungs, though collapsed, were birds. My lungs, though collapsed, were monuments of feathers. The voices wind a heavy preponderance of holography. Sensation is alive with a woman's waist. An umbrella of eyes winks beneath the faucets, letting dreams dribble along the slender waist, along the swollen thigh, along the forest of night where lips wait for the dawn to drive them from decay. The swallows in the walls are hermetic whispers and pearl inset within the eye's pupil to create a voice of clouds. Stairways like the voices that penetrate my belly. A hole in the hole where shadows linger possess their shadow's finger. A night of crows and there are no hand rails, only smoke to cling to.

The soft pillow of dawn possesses me like a clinging knife in the cupboards of sweet whispers. It is the moon's relaxation that eclipses the sun's overbearing hunger. I count hundreds of intentions with their wavering glass blades that lick to and fro like a pendulum. Across the eyelids, a fish swims with arms whose fleshy milkiness is a parade of hallucinated dreams of wet fire. Ice crystals and domes of vision are scarcely out of the passage of view when they intertwine in a dance of moths. Their feelers wield their gowns of translucent whispers. Interiors are far beyond the spectral of light, far beyond the measure of silence and far beyond the dark underbelly of the centipede's silver circle. The interiors are warm, and at the end of that are a Mozambique canvas and a pearl casket. The sharp remark is from silence's quivering pale monologue. Time is incandescent, and it is also a spiral watch. To descend or to ascend the stairway's darkness is a parade of costly tongues.

"The Plain"

"Enter the moon of the second part," a voice suddenly burst like fire. "The moon of the second part, Osiris is searching for his bodily remains amongst the reeds and the desert sands." I smell the smell of hay burning upon my eyelids. I look and see a man dressed in brown pajamas coming my way. I await his arrival, counting the burns in the sky.

"Ho," I call out to him. "Where are you going, and why the unusual dress?" He passed me by, saying nothing, but dragging his entrails behind him. He was the dreamy pestilence of fish. The fog of thick walls surrounds the medieval dance, and I am alone skirting the sand's sweet song. The dry mouth searches the sky for a moist tongue. Where birds hide, fountains express their desire. Boxes of burning secrets are those desires. The sun is forgotten in its linen of crossed legs. A mass of thighs has crossed an ill-gotten dream on a sea of fish that are frozen voices and a magic of sumptuous time. I cry out like the night's robe. Grains of whispered salt are the arms that swim, and the plaster face explodes where birds migrate. The straightjackets of magician otters entreat a pleasure for a parade. The forgotten paradises of pleasures sit in the elevator of eyes sinking deep into a moist mouth.

I felt that I must follow the man dragging his entrails, but something gripped my heart. As he disappeared, I saw a faint outline of a paint brush in the sky. I sat and watched as the clouds unfolded their arms, and the brush moved in a slow dance.

"The Painting"

A bird's beak could not pluck from the sky a more delicate wish. The fleeting moment of silent whispers is a stroke of green on Surat's flesh. I have listened to the gentle flow of water passing over my chest in a guarded fashion. Silence awakened the star's ears. Some mysterious hand has reached up and struck a torch to the sky, setting the clouds aflame and letting loose a thunder of voices that asks for directions to the fallen mill. What could have been taken for nuns, were actually penguins huddled near the railway station. They were waiting for their hunger to be brought down with the shades. Darkness and a painting of the moon beside the moon, it was a picture of a woman's lips hidden in the crevasse of my own lips like a foaming tongue of the ocean. A picture of a word making love to the swollen rubber in unseen places under the breast where the moon only goes out at night.

The seductive clouds that hang in the air resemble a bandage over an immense wound. My eyes have lifted themselves from my face and stand with the birds on the horizon. A picture of an old man is weeping into a cave. There are little stones arranged in the form of symbols at his feet. The picture has some words written across the sky, "Les Temps du Poisson." The whole painting can be misconstrued as a fable, a mythical applause, and a magical dance of squares or a motion of movement sounding out unheard whistles. Hyenas howl in the distance; by the sound of their voices I know that their shadows resemble roosters. Wolves awaken in the briars beneath my pillow that I carry in my arm.

The seasons, the stars and the breathing sky are a moment all pressed in the quarter of the hand that is as small as a bird's wing. A voice from out of the depths is cold as the abyss of shadowed whispers. I parade them amongst the foil's reflection. The soft whisper of a stone floor angles out in a direction that only droplets of blood can follow. The myth cannot be complete without the aura of Oros and the dance of a thousand moons faces the hovering bed of iron. Fortune cast its left eye into a black hole, and rabbits speak loudly about the horned frost. The moon, the black moon, never is silver under a night of blood. Its brilliance only comes after the sacrifice, and then only with leather shoes.

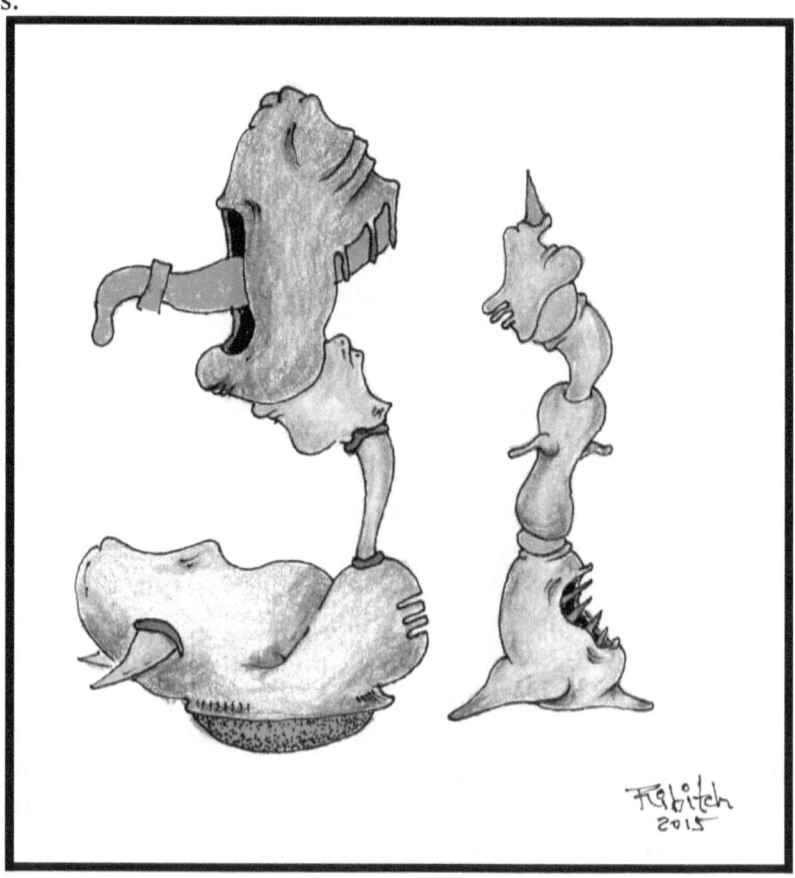

NOTHING TO BE AFRAID OF IN THE DARK

Slipping a tongue into the air, a moment or two perhaps, is laid upon a woman's shoulders of fine silk. The blood that ran like rivers across the chest reveals a not too dogmatic face that howls in laughter and frays the sky with lips of razors. It was at this moment in heat and foam, the dancer's quay made of silk, swayed far out into the horizon, not linking the milk of the earth to the starry winks of a wolf sky. A dancer's jest is full of opalescent globules of dust, of meager lust beyond the shoulders of dusk. I can sit and listen to the silent array of jets of blood. The foaming heart that is taken in my hand pushes through the walls of my chest to where waiting eagles thirst in hunger for the warmth of my pallet. Discreet, the poison of salt lifts a head to whisper something in an audible tone, something that plants a seed of fire beneath the sea's clavicle womb. My own voice, not at all hidden, speaks in the silent tones that often are given over to wolves, which can form into doorways that are jaws filled with discreet lines of grain, but are bloody with the fresh kills that stain the floor.

The night leans upon stationary platforms stroking a crucifix, only to snap it in two. It beguiles the flesh of the moon to move one more inch closer to the eyes that perceive it. The eyes swallow it in one mighty gulp. The eyes rape the glow and fill it with a night of pleasure. The night, that night, or any other night is wild with the excitement that freezes blue a music of fingers that playfully extract the sun's vocal membranes, teasing them to drown in the dark ponds of flesh and magic.

Dark whispers of the flesh brood in the wings of caprice. Whispers that haunt the dawn cannot hide beneath its skirts of bright flame. Whispers of the oven turned hot on the back of the eyelids to reveal birds of silver, reflecting solicitations and taunting voices. Would the jungle take its arms from around the heart, to beat away the bearing flights of snakes? The beads of sweat on a lost arm took its flight into unheeding mystery. No mystery or fold of soft silence touches the lips that wine gives way to. Darkness takes over the folds of a black curtain over the mouth. No shouts penetrate its folds. No necessary light will filter through its eyes of silt. No airy grayness from one horizon to another horizon, just the night in the spectacles of radiant blackness. A jungle in Bangor, its leaves cut off the waking vision of light. Darkness so possessed with the laughter of night's jaw. Pupils expand beyond the vertical limitations of the head. Darkness whispers that there are no more airy snaps of bones crying out the sleek secrets of a salamander's back, that is set with a fire of gloves and a slipping tongue halfway into the air to grasp at a woman's breast flying in the wind as dark as childhood.

PERSPECTIVES!

There is an incredible surge of something hazy that entwines through the vestibule of thought, as though a plate of armor extended to the low places that sift and filter the earth with fingers of feathers. The distended sky, like flesh, like an open wound that resembles the face of a man who resembles not the breath of the forest. It was in this impeccable mood in which I found the house that stood as if it were a stone that stood with its eves reaching out like hands toward the filled space of my shadow. It was a large house. It had lungs. It was sided by a very tall parapet from which hung the frayed rope of a former occupant. His sadness was a grape. I could hear the breathing of the vines, but only my tongue could envelope them. The doorway was hidden by a large hand, whose only vocation toward the root was the foliage at its base and an indefinable house, like ink sewn to the sky.

Like the impressions of a tropical land, at first unseen in their uncanny appearance, the whispers of hidden faces stand within the foundations of something extra-translucent. The fog of hair that surrounds the antiquity of that motion stands in front of a house, holding a fossil of former age, like tattoos upon its skin. A stone walkway leads to the house, and it too is imprinted through the grip of desire, at the point of departure, at the point of entry, at the point of an instant shiver that consumes the walls, where the spirit craves defiance.

At certain hours, the veil of the air creeps. This is my image. This is the seriousness of the implantation of the roots of shadows. So I pass on, letting the hours of the night guide me. It is only as the night can do, letting the cameo of its appearance whisper with a voice strengthened by the bearing of the frost. The coated veil and the hidden mandrill in the guise of a snail, posed the mind set of frosted infinities, like the glass cocoon, from which utter the screams of something totally visible.

A sign at the end of the path foretold of something beyond the festooned walls of the haphazard flesh. A sign at the end of the path foretold to me, and only to me, the secrets of its parting flesh; something quite beyond the mounting shadows; something that was staged for my eyes only. It's an invisible, yet highly visible play of alluring antiquities. As the sign read before my eyes like a blood vessel, burst in an enduring display up my visceral passage. Like laughter, the words were scrolled, "Marveilleux: House of Parades, House of Poisons and the Unnatural Acts, J.T. Mouten, Proprietor and General Influence."

No amount of resistance can persuade the levels of the water to recede. Their grip is insistent and wholly persuasive in the deluge of the moment's passion. It is a monstrous explosion or an exposition of strangers, who for the price of the night, steal the snails from their shells and paste them to the sky. No amount of resistance, not even the fear-possessed night, can persuade the levels of the water to recede; nor shall halt the inclusion of desire beyond the carved walls of this ancient mausoleum. So I enter and face the possibilities of the grand farce and the presence of something staged in its laughter.

The door, a huge panel that could have been woven, swings on its hinges like a bat. The air was dense, but not explosive. The drone of the atmosphere almost swallowed the entire night. The encompassed hinges swallowed the air in great gulps. The grain of the wood and the landscapes of women's thighs lay just beyond the opening, an opening beyond the beyond, an opening into the delightful intrusion of the footsteps of my shadow leaning toward the darkness. The illusion of fear is testing my tongue. The shadows of voices that crowd the entrance of so many dreams are like a fog that holds my hand. I felt the door shut behind like a shudder. I could smell the smell of wolves with its passing breeze. I could feel the brush of lions on their passing. The darkness was thick in my mouth. The dust on the floor was like wasps beneath my feet and it was conjugating the migration of my breath to the walls. The afternoon can only be ellipsed by the degrees in which it is frozen along the road.

The swollen tigers and their broods come along the pathway that catches sight with their tails, all the mammals within the leaves. I can smell a woman in the room by her hair, the season's convulsions and a storm. It is raining inside, even though the roof is solid. It could be believed that the room was as any other room, a highly conferrable fact, were it not for a certain laughter that scaled off the walls as a sensuous pleasurable laughter, like dreams in their wetness. It is the laughter hidden in the groin of a lion. I could not make up my mind, from which direction the laughter made its appearance first. What was the merit of its description? Was it a glass empirical or the worn tooth from the rug's finest array? For sure, its deception was a chameleon on a leaf; the urge to alight like the sheerest of dreams caught within the hailstones of some future development dissolved in such delusion as the light played itself off the wall, the skirts of its madness was listening. On the verge of sudden discovery, an open womb like a vessel of china pottery, glistening and waiting the sound of an explosion. The die is cast and forever caught in the prism in its insistence.

Man fell from the sky as a worm and in that state shivered through the shifting balance of his brain. Silence could not be his, for voices of his birth and forthcoming death could not cease its mingling track across his consciousness. Even his calloused fingers could not rip from his brain all that consumed him. With magic and dream the fortunes of his house were made. In the light of distilled air, all that came within reach was encompassed within the cells of madness, like a fragment of suddenness. The architectural structure, the leaves of the morning, like the fine hairs of some reflection, cast a shadow where only dreams dare invade. To the end of the earth, the wink of an eye is a shadow of consuming walls of digested thought, the sensation of reflection, of conjunction and migration. The passage and the flogging of the thought of disappearance lays beneath the fog! With tomorrow's rains, the sea has exploded in tiny crystals. To the end of the hall, to the end of the space is where trees turn into birds and my mind sits in dream waiting.

THIRD MORNING

The aftermath of a metallic fog

it's full of cat screams!

What are left behind are the translucent voices.

An image of trap doors with their hinges gone crazy

behind such laughter so full

that it fills deep cankerous wells.

A piece of cloth seems to gauge the air

with its voice of whispered crows.

Silence intertwined itself in the moon of essence and snow.

Half hollow hands that greet the flash of death

are yielding their promise of profane mud.

They laugh with their reflection of sonnets.

My feet with snails tied to them,

bid good night, with all the austerity

the budding future will allow.

What future can there be

when my teeth of varmints

are stealing the aftermath of a conclusion?

They are ripped from beneath my nails

and sold for bottles of water.

The thin air is coughing with flames.

Weeding the needle tough the eye of the bear,

the saga of sanity runs itself to the back of blackness

like a split wrist of a doll.

The wall of seething flame is moist in the sandwiched air.

Smoke of persistent air, strips the belly's flesh

and is harmful to the ears of cats.

The Cabala full of worms

and castrates three minstrels in women's clothing.

The moist running of blood in the street

is full of naked revealing signposts,

like the sarcophagus of serpent wanderings.

A bird disguised itself as a flaming beard of snow,

it cuts with a tooth knife all the bloody pickerels.

The dawn is twice as benevolent as its cousin,

attached to the frayed wall like a decomposed balloon.

This dawn, soiled by the fragrance of death.

So sad, the dawn that sits upon my eyelids.

It has become a morning of flame.

The crescent of oblivion above a bed of meal worms,

castrates the fewer of centuries

that grapple with the translucent worms.

The naked crest of volume blundered

in wonder of sideshow attractions.

There is a peekhole oblivion

where the geek stands within his scrotum.

His tail in his hand like an oval disk,

he wanders with fishhooks and marmalade fat ladies.

Judas is bleeding on a marble platform,

Muttering to himself the obituaries of fallen flags

and their attempted ascensions to the cross.

Stones and faces are marking the path of sailboat women.

The leaves of their breasts are contagious

with the swelling of their hearts.

Stripped of their ambivalence like a sword

hung above their heads,

they embrace the wound of heaven in their groins.

The flag masters and masturbators

are curling under their own flesh,

like ants under the tombs of headstones.

The full height of the wire is executing the neck.

Swarms of fish are under dry conditions,

maximizing their strength to crack the globe of their hearts.

The empress of glass fog,

the sweet vibrant cells of her virgin whisper

extend the vestments of her warmth.

The bleeding nail falters

on the brink of sanity like a mirror.

The placid waters with an undergrowth of legs

is second to the hallway of blossoms.

The visitant in hostile perfume

is like a chemise boat of masks.

Brain damage, a discharge in a lake of gallows

is swarming like bees over the flesh.

Running from a herd of stampeding phrases

is the exhuming black back of deliverance.

The oval mask of blistered saints,

who without the exponent of frailty,

dissipate with a gust of breath

There was an accident that swallowed the womb.

The fire in the ice is returning to haunt the horizon.

The strings of circumstance

are brothels awakening to the dead.

To the land, a land of bloody boots.

The worried cry of dusk

takes the worn sleeves of the future

To beat them into rags.

Bloody boots that worn by children

are displayed like frozen death spores

on the countless remains of whispered grief.

They are crucified to the wanting development,

that sensation in its excruciating display

folds into a vomiting bird.

Crystal faces and red leaves of bone

snuggled against the tapestries that gargoyles molest.

The sweaters of fawns are turning inward

to the centimeters of oblivion's door.

The door smells of penguin and urgent genital windows.

The door opens onto the grey horizon filled with smoke.

The bagpipes of frost gather in the meadows to die.

There must, in all ambiguity,

cease to be a silence that is quicksilver.

Bone beds are lying naked in Egyptian swamps,

where lovers congregate in the spray of seaweed veils.

They lay in a casket of roses,

to seep in the vivacity of phosphorus sun.

Glass sensations are breathing explosions.

Duck wings cry loud and vibrant

with the will of the past in open portals.

Expedient sand, floss and bran,

the hour has arrived for extra wounds.

Doorways that laugh!

The esophagus stretched toward oblivion

like a sack of nails.

Nails of the philosopher's stone

are protruding from swamp mud.

Too many offspring are hovering

in the shadows of a distant reminder,

like hawks of black women sailing

Their feet like emotions.

The bird of hell sits at the breakfast table

with its homecoming visitation of a plate of roses.

The velvet vase of prudent smiles

are squalid masks of frost devils.

Irredeemable mouths open to a vacant summit.

A world of wildebeest and dead fawns

are milking a deflated sun, striking a plate glass

and a wreath of vellum dogmas.

The extraction of violent teeth

that top the moon with open lips,

separates the tongue from the wall

where the morning fails to flourish.

There is no exception to the space

lost in the separateness of strange delusions.

The despondence that lies on the flagstones

amongst the scream of spiderweb faces.

It is being emptied of the ashes

and the bones of the unaware.

The indifferent perambulation into a backward mirror

is set in rust and wrapped in lace like a shroud of queens.

Beaded angels wrapped themselves

in the flurried sensation of obscene vespers;

their tunics are torn from their bodies.

Who are the fools that succumbed to their deaths?

They are like beds in the window

that call out to the winter's fulmination.

There is nothing beneath their eyelids.

This is a question that is answered

in all the convents that bleed

beneath black veils and whispers.

The question too sprouts wings of ice

and flees on the somber tongues that utter it.

The columns of marble are like spoonfuls of water.

The plastic utterance that displays

sentries of reflections.

Standing on the cowardice of mutable faces,

whose only deliverance is the dawn.

Something that extracts itself from the poison

of a severed waist turns about like a ghost in the hall.

Singled out in bitter seclusion,

a single faceless face is sewn onto a marble.

it is growing on a cloud of seamless affirmations,

like a moss that swallows the glazing touch.

A beam of fire is wired to the blast furnace.

Stones are laid in the pathway of armchairs

who call out in the ecstasy of a passionate summer.

Calling out of doors that are made out of rubber,

that they may mold themselves

into the closet clowns of the dawn.

Minutes of the clock respond

to the alleyways of demands.

One moment is flexing to the next with a sailor's hand.

A year of days bleeds in their fellows' coffins.

Every passion is extended like an ascended hand.

The year of my birth

displayed the hour of my death,

like a swath of gummy film over the eyes.

Budding futures displayed themselves in glass tubes,

where the year of my birth

marks the beginning of the firestorm

for filling in the desperate moments of infinity.

The cages are growing ears to hear the breaking day.

The mammoth configuration of the stars

is stealing the breath from a child's wounded heart.

The present matter of thought

is hidden in a veil of muses,

liquid in their sublime presence.

A year in this morning is twice in the eye,

asking the pristine waking breath cascade

to hold itself with a blander interest.

A fog of bereaved women is like a lizard's back,

wavering as the ship of their thighs.

Their mouths are swallows' nests vested in oblivion.

This is the century of the malignant gossamer of a glance.

The oval glazing of the past

is seen through the shimmering wanderings of water mirrors.

Voices who disclaim their clarity

with prismatic osculation.

The variance of concordance of blood

that blackbirds with their covenant of little metal hands,

milk the chasm of its darkness,

lifting the rails of bondage

and extracting the gluttonous flames that will to cinder.

Even after the dust of mosses has cleared the nostrils,

the fingers of migrant strength conclude on an evening

that is frayed with iron oxide scrapings.

That all that is displayed, is also hidden

with the reaper in the afternoon

of bloodied spurs and triangle hearts.

There is a breech in the perception of the dawn

like an old boat rushing into hell.

Voluminous worms are undressing

under platforms of wounded women.

Stone blinds are executing the expectant visions.

True to their forms they lapse into their misfortunes.

There are bullet holes in the soft membranes of time's blood.

Onions covered the walls of oblivion's toast.

Seaweed willows with fingers of women's legs

unfold in their magic reflection of vacant moods.

A blackened scream is deadened by all the leaves

that are compressed by the frost.

The budding ears are staged on a platform of ice,

their wings of granite caterpillars are grasping the wind.

The pitted wall is disguised in the folds of a face.

The black wings of beauty,

like a claw, is slashing the sun.

Walking in a backward motion,

it is lapping the billows of black across the hand.

Some strange sigh concludes existence like a drop of water.

Consider it weakminded in a wind of abuses.

Singed to the bone and waterlogged up to the neck,

nothing is as sweet as to parade sensation

above the level of skirted stars.

Singing the blues from a burning building,

the flaming insurrection is curved

in the ballast of silence.

The pearlhandled waistline

that possesses women of bloody birds,

they have all thrown their panties into cesspools.

They have all followed them down,

for that day was theirs.

The numbers of the veil

are bursting bubbles of passion

and are sending out images of lips

that scandalize their request.

A plague of mastodons

And the vital necessity of the violent act,

Pleads with the rain that

soaks the fibers of the jealous pachyderms.

Their bloody knees are doing battle with the frost.

Their heirs of stimulations and confusions

are laid across their breast

like the poisonous hips of dead women.

These same mammoth beasts thought to be extinct,

scream across in a morning filled with flame.

The same dead thighs

That cut from the moon a silver glass

and the cold reminder of dawn's fingers.

Solomon in his grave of stagnated moss

is singing out with a voice

that is heavily weighted with dust

and silent running futures.

futures that will see no tomorrows,

because the dawn is burning.

Lizards have made their nest

within the brocade of heaven

and within the brocade of heaven,

the fiery walls of an aimless carnival.

Shreds of the calliope mourn

beneath the corollas of sleep.

The dryness of the wind is reaping

the bones of whales,

who threw their hernias to the ground,

where children sleep under them.

The whispers of such children collide

And mingle with the stolen hats of their grandfathers.

There is a fine growth of hair

that screams of automobiles.

From Salem, the rain and the sign of dust

wield about in the canopy of the wind.

The Flamboyant call of the molested window.

Even the seasons are weeping in its bloody splendor

to ask for a shadow and a glimpse of the moon's underside.

The face is wrestled from the vortex

of some false illusion

and the dancing bears from Salem

stand in the rain and eye the glass of rippled words.

The amorous touch of outlaw winds

that has squandered away the night's breath

in an ocean of promise, like a chandelier of whispers

too silent to repose upon the knees of the sky.

The barely discernible winter

and the crow's valor pressed against the sun,

they have seen themselves reflected

in the shallows of the morning.

Birds sing their shadows on the path of the future.

The morning is drunk, but not more drunken than I.

The reflection that has refused to see

is melted in a cast of swirled silences.

The token catatonic smiles invade

The mirrored place,

like stones that bleed under its touch.

To clock away the demon time,

whose voice is distilled in the mangled bush,

the dawn swallows in the haste of far-reaching futures.

It is too militant for the frost

to gather around its waist something squandered

by the false alleys of the dormant wind.

Are those dying cherubs too sweet to swallow,

to be counted amongst the Sabine frogs?

Each end is its own pillow.

The breath has risen and attached its sailor's mouth,

without hesitation to unfamiliar silences.

With each moment the prepared cloud whispers are,

full of blood,

full of nervous action,

full of fish in the air.

The bloody moon has sliced the face of the sun.

The bleeding moon is a hawk's fevered lust.

I have bitten into all of the layers

that coat the ghostly past,

even the shoulders that stare

into some child's rotted mouth.

For every inch of the nervous sky

that is waiting to excite its breath,

it will see to all the hats that rise with the dawn.

Open the bitter stairways!

The sun has changed its clothes

in a room full of smoking ambiences.

The frail porters are packing off bags

of the past, wrapped in leather and ostrich feathers.

Declining any comment of discourse,

the clocks have refused their winders

and have sold to the haunches of the wind all their years.

Black owls and masks of lead

are laid out in the snow in neat little rows.

The crying trails are filled with polished stone

and the etched face of a whistling dog.

My appearance on the horizon

is a shadow painting the moon with icy fingers.

My appearance is sucking mold

from the sky like rotting wood.

All my breath is in the wind,

searching the grooves for reflections of an appearance

and my appearance of snow

is collecting the phantoms of rage.

There is a secret laughter

that haunts the song of egrets.

Laughter in caves that silence consumes.

This morning that approaches on dog feet,

swallows the moon with eager delight.

The motion of my hand is extreme in the violence

that is a dog's ear in a closet of sperm.

My voice consumes the remnants

of the night with eager teeth.

My appearance waxes and wanes

like a shadow murdered under the moon.

My appearance is a bloodied knife

when all the crows with their frozen hearts

sit upon my appearance of snow.

Each counts the tiny hairs

that cling to my eyelids

and each one is a reflection

of bone drowning in the seas of death.

A voice that excites the succulent palms of my hands

also vomits in the corner on stones of ambivalent rage.

Speak to me!

Speak to me, so that my throat may swallow.

Stretch out arms of ancient corollas

that wander through the seaweed of dawn.

Place upon a weeping stone,

the crows of sex

and under it a bottle of memories.

Then set fire to the dolls,

whose hands are stained with the ejaculations

of blood, wine and spit.

The babies' breath smells of whiskey and spit.

The soft fat tummies that lay open are revealing

the iron works of dead birds and soft entrails.

These babies, who in rigor mortis

fall beneath the flames

that settle at their feet,

flesh out the silk of wings.

The worms that invade their entrails

Are of glass and silence.

The floorboards,

stained with the rich milk of their blood

are the songs of silence.

The hum of ancient whispers

are like an eclipse of the wings of a thousand insects.

These babies, who are dressed in iron feathers

are all sporting mustaches.

All the silent whispers of death

hop on all fours

bringing this platitude of extreme violence

into the open on a cask of vaporous mouths.

Whisper to me the litanies of crazed ambiguity.

This, my body, filled with Yucca moths,

it too steals the mask of wooden futures.

The ants of glass fibers hide beneath my navel.

The nervous quake that trembles

beneath my eyelids like a hallucination of stone,

laughs with a hunter's hand.

The extreme laughter that spins

in the cry that is nestled in my teeth

is the rabid floatation of dark closets.

My ascent into a scream is full of pain

felt deep within the collar bone.

All the doorways lead into the third morning.

A morning of hung nuns.

A morning of hats,

parading with their pompous heads.

A morning where faces

peel themselves from mirrors.

The coughing bull has slit its own throat

to see if it is made of clay.

In the spilling of blood,

the face up against the wall

howls for the morning to shed its garments

with woman-like hands,

shedding the silk and all silence like a tomb.

The remnants of a thousand overcoats

parade themselves into the dawn.

The dancing monkey takes the silver plate

to fling it skyward,

where the slow motion of the mongoose

irritates the glass eye of a metaphor.

In every dark room paradise is filled

with suicide and gaily colored musicians.

There is laughter in a room of dampness,

where tears fill the fish bowl,

where the humming bird has drowned.

The air is filled with overcoats,

from which everywhere the eye falls

there are torn pockets

and from the tweed sleeves protrude

the bony realities of severed hands.

This dawn of the monkey's paw

where second sight reveals itself

in the tiny crevasses of madness and birth.

The dawn of worms with bird beaks and lace eyes.

The dawn of formal wear,

hung by the neck and swinging by the still-visible moon.

The dawn that clings

to the testicles of the hermaphrodite sky,

swallows the full measure of its own excrement.

This dawn that laughs and weeps in the same moment.

This dawn that sits on my eyelids like an old man.

This dawn of war, the dawn of the third morning.

Seaweed skies grope at the little hands

that tap on the pavement.

Swollen dead hands of plastic dolls.

The sidewalk is full of dolls

wearing Carmen Miranda hats and lace tutus

The doll's arms don't work anymore,

but hang loose like wires.

Their eyes are eternally open

or else they are closed

They don't see anyway,

but snicker at the bloody sky,

where everything falls around their feet like mold.

Robins adorn their hair like splotches of blood.

Their plastic skin rises to butcher the remaining moon.

The dolls hunger resembles

the frozen buttress of playful silhouettes,

For all this I run, but my legs don't follow.

The scallop that clings

to the sky like a horned mollusk

traps the oncoming sun in a cupped proboscis.

Icecream waists wander about

finding interludes for my heart of bicycle's laments.

The fluttering hair

that hangs from my lips like cold ice,

talks of the dirigible wind and broken bird.

There are butterfly teeth

hung from the fronds of a deliberate frost.

The broken vocal cords belong to armadillo elephants.

All of the dancing spiders

with their pork stuffed furniture

allude to the balloon makers of Accad,

who eat breakfast atop mount Ararat

with naked dolls, who gaze

with gazelle eyes and frothing mouths.

My fingers of Rumanian rubber,

like my heart of sensational poison,

like my feet of claws and nuptial hammers

are pounding out the time worn clocks

that hurry to the articulated dawn.

Burning branches that hang from the sky,

like old bones that hang from the waist.

My fingers spring in the air,

grabbing the stars from their beds of nails

and I fling them beneath my shirt of ice.

The orifice of compliance

stretched to the horizon like a mangled bull,

excites the gracious tombs

that fall beneath the weight of the obstinate dead.

Kingdoms of fish conclude

their dreadful adventure beneath the butcher's blade.

They haunt the tumbleweed forest

like a phosphorous cloud,

like a poisonous dart of Matis hunter's dream.

Melded upon ancient fingers,

my skin elopes with Moroccan frogs

They tie one eye to the next

and unfold the blankets of summer

where they stand on the edge of smoke.

The weight of cancerous years stand

in the vast hallways of the paranoid host.

His dreams are salamanders

crawling across placid eyes.

Fingers that search outside their gloves,

bereaving the frost,

are lost within the tango of the heart.

Dance upon the razor of clouded histories.

Dance upon my face of bitter wine.

Dance like the cockatoo's navel,

where flesh meets flesh

and death is a stain on my tongue.

The night has eluded all reason

by riding on the back of a tortoise

like a reflection of a torn sleeve.

The street lamp mocks

the marsupial shadow of passing bones,

each turns a magnet of failing strength

and pilfers the staid thirst,

like the moment of detachment

when the rose with its breath of coal

Concludes its season of dream

and whispers a tune with the lute,

the loon and the frost.

The sauntering passage of time

is like an endless shadow of the wolverine moon.

The woman's breast of night,

where feet moan a clandestine cry,

they are humming their litanies

to the grey whale carcass

that sits at a bus stop of dawn.

Their flesh like my flesh burns

As the tourniquet of possible intervention

finds repose in the escaping vellum of sleep.

Crying out of black sleep,

blood red sleep,

sleep of icicle stars,

in a bedroom of snails and floating jars of sperm,

it is there that my eyes execute the plains of ejaculation.

There are frozen bicycles

coming to dance in the parade.

To see that dance as an execution of frozen thought,

is to see the moment of sublime interlude

caught within the lion's jaw.

Queen of spades in a gypsy moon!

Moon of gypsy spades

caught in dangerous romance!

Flight of buzzards,

their bicycles have all turned to flame,

to light up a night of twilight sparrows.

This is a fortunate blaze of burning chairs.

Queen moon in a gypsy's hair!

Moths of dreams and silence

are thrown over the precipice of autocratic delusion.

Static dream,

queen illusion,

the fragrant mist of shadows growing.

Silent queen in death ravels,

melting in the royal blood of satiety.

The open mouth of screams on sea of ears

is the flood of steaming gratitude

hung from the air like African boar frogs.

Night of silent queens

who have all swallowed their tongues.

This night of gypsy moon.

The sparrow's fire is sudden and full of jackals.

The moment of the bird's romance

is wed to the abyss of laughing dogs.

There are clowns in their Arabian thunder

and they are sweeping up in their coat of snails.

The piers are full of weeping women,

their arms of lace lie molded at their sides.

The fish that trail behind them

escort an idea, or else fly on the winds.

From the beginning the face of the leper

encased in ice was so silent

when approaching the dream sparrow

that the fall wind was caught

crying out of its plastic breath.

When it came to the owl's madness,

all that was left was his shadow,

nailed to the wall of his cranium

like all of his dreams.

Those dreams of naked futures

are filed in a lead box as if they were ears.

Silent dreams invade

the secret passages of his heart.

The stone cubicle of his eye

is where nature has slit her throat.

Ah! Bloody moon on the surface,

the waistline of fear has taken my hands

and sewn them to the ears of saints.

This is my plague, my passion!

It appears as a woman's face

and vanishes as a fog.

Silent frost succumbs

to the laughter of a hunter's snow.

My ears of boar's intestines

hear the coming feet of parading wolves

and their dreams of ice.

They freeze the well documented anemia of the well,

where all the drowned visions

remove their clothes and weep

in the foil of their nakedness.

There is a song of motion in a wind of rats,

twirling aloft in the soft under petals

of this illusory breath.

Come into my dream arms, madness,

vision of moths with iron arms.

The glass breast is held aloft

within the fronds of reason.

My eyes of hornets and broken bones

want for that sleep,

that slumbers,

that quietude of ancient frost.

Succumbing to my waist of crustaceans,

the ropes of writhing sounds are the limitation

that the coming morning has hung.

So silent is the rage of vomiting suns,

encased in rapture and clung to the ceiling

with apelike hands,

that its face lies hidden within a chemise.

The sounds of gulls wax in the sky.

The hot breath of silt and lava

is hunting the moon's frayed mouth

with whispers as sweet as death

and as haunting as a jeweled mist.

My bed of conical thorns

hovers above the horizon.

The shade of its presence

is a dried leaf sitting on a woman's shoulders.

My bed of Egyptian dreams

is hidden beneath the stars

where sleep is never taken on my bed of ospreys.

There is a fragrant rope of lips hung

about my neck in garlands

that is heavy in the aroma of garlic.

Every afternoon peels back their skins,

revealing my ears on the hearth

and my teeth glowing in the mist of dream.

Dreams, the closure of ancient doors.

Pulling back the curtain

on the grappling sons of death,

my soul of mirrors is reflecting

the turn of the age

and the dawn of pearlescent landscapes.

My feet are glued to water,

so that no shadow in this well of illusion falls,

nor does the dust of children's hands.

Standing by itself in a sheath of rain,

my shoulders wear the chrysalis wrapped in fog

and steals the hour of morning breath.

To count naked upon my hands,

the bones of some laughter,

those bones of discreet dissolution.

those bones purified under a crescent sun.

All the undaunted

are held in a hunter's hand,

like a sack of snow on the back of tomorrow

that capitulates to the coughs of the dead.

Upon a platform of stolen whispers,

the sticks of illusion drown under the fell.

The burning hats where the sea ends

play on mandolins the songs of cadavers.

Their corollas are boats of humming birds.

The crying dogs that lash themselves

to the wind are breathing with punctured lungs.

All their futures hang on the edge of the dawn

like a chrysalis of bone.

The matted hair that clings to the face of the sky,

clotted in blood and confusion,

wields its baneful breath,

slicing the grandeurs of dream.

The tombs that years have passed unobserved,

with all their stolen little honey cakes

are nailed to babies whose futures are ice

under the flame of the human crucible.

The dreamer utters out like an umbrella.

The passersby who watch the dream

with dust-covered feet

can't speak any longer,

because they have passed

under the bridges of flirtation.

The caustic remarks,

oh slumber unheeded,

that daybreak of sturgeons,

that hour of the third morning

when all the shoes have left their masters

and the dream has not yielded.

It is my voice,

my lips,

my haunting heartbeat,

under a moon of vestibules,

where the howling lays claim to your slumber.

Under this moon of delirious bays,

the axiom of chance

lays forth the hunger of thought.

Under this moon,

my moon,

moon of human lungs,

there lie the secret spiral whispers of silence.

The silence that clogs my lungs with spider webs,

Finds its solitude with the hermaphrodite winds.

The silence of my ears

when they chase dogs in the night!

Is this my voice,

my lips and crab claw hats

that peel the skin of the earth,

revealing the blueness of its mouth.

My mouth, like the mouth of the earth

howls within the reverberation of the dawn.

The water of the sea falls skyward,

to blanket the moon with velvet hands.

The inhabitants of that ancient flow

are punctured by that crescent

that swings upon the slates of time,

and time alone in its monolithic stare

intrudes where the whale's rotting carcass

Plays dominos with aquatic vertebrates.

How many ships lie rusted

At the bottom of the sky?

Or the roof of the sea?

How much rust in the cornea of the eye

that sops at the conch shell?

The sands conclude their travels

with haunting clarity,

each voicing the extreme preponderance of satiety.

The fish wait for transportation,

bus or heated balloon,

while the salt of the air

lies in the bed of the mundane.

Shreds of broken glass fill the rooms

where little doll's arms laugh out in their hysteria.

The faces that frown out from the windows,

powdered white and pasted pink from rouge,

seek out hidden pleasures

that remain behind elastic grins.

The plastic face of policemen crack

where the morning's wind

exposes their naked genitals.

Their pricks have been cut from their waist

and hang loose from their broken necks

like the flags that hang limp from their scrotums.

Herring bone waistcoats

wait upon the black neckties

hoping for the incriminating circumstances

to reveal themselves as little blocks of stone

or slivers of skin.

This is heat hung in exposure with such wilted shadows.

The reflections that slide off their mirrors

with careening madness is this,

the dawn of seminal misfortune.

Unexpected rushes of delirium

howls with the trembling scent of wolves

and their passion for blood.

The stone of ambiance,

where frogs hunt out their own skins,

peeling them back above their eyelids of jade.

Those frost-cornered eyelids

where women lay sewn to their beds

like sheets of the wind.

Frost-covered eyelids

that fill trenches with the bones of slate.

Hollow semen of broken glass

that evades its season,

the November thunder of man,

who in the likeness of death

erodes under the rain.

The rapine wind

that seeks to conclude the eve of storms,

follows the night into alleys of dream.

The stream of dark pearl is black

where the night ends.

The breath that clings to winter's hooves

cries out with a severed throat.

The millennium of the dawn,

whose blood-filled shoes

is a whistle cutting the chalk-filled night.

Shrill screams fill fountains of bathtubs,

their skins are leprous tumors on the moon.

Those sweet cadavers, like candy sticks

waltz in halftime with roses as cold as their death.

So slow is the movement of their sallow lips,

that death rides a wild wind.

A horse whose corpse flesh eludes reason,

is draped in blood,

coughing spittle and choked in mud.

My face is peeled back revealing

the bones of my nakedness

like a swallow butchered by a grin.

My breath with weights of gravel

is indeed heavier than the stones

at the foot of my bed,

each was a labor of painful transfiguration,

as my face is muzzled

beneath the blankets of chain.

My bed of stolen sobs

has fled to the sea to drown

next to crabs who grip their futures,

like my eyes,

like my sleep beneath their bellies filled with moss.

This bed of mine that jackals turn over in their hands.

Their knuckles bleed rivers into my dreams.

Those dreams that cling to my lips like snow on my neck.

Each sleep is mirrored in hysteria.

The sleep of owls,

The sleep of shadows hung upon hooks

and red wine is hung from them.

The silent sleep of moles eaten by wolves

or stripped of their skins.

This sleep enchained within the shackles of insomnia.

My pillow hides beneath the waves of sweet distress,

allowing their bellies to open up like fish.

I cry in the wake of sleep

that hides like a drum in horrible solitude.

It alludes to fingers that are yellow in death.

My tongue is placed within a thimble,

Covered with a shroud

and carried through the streets of monolithic flesh.

Is this forgotten, the guttural cry?

The floor seems so far away

To be mentioned by my hardened mouth.

Those lovely little fingers of death

Hang by the moon,

their fingers broken

by the weight of their dramas.

What makes the words taken

by their vocal cords fall from the sky like bones?

The figurines of glass are frozen

to the ceiling of my mouth.

The screams that resemble faces

are detached and frozen to the umbilical of some dream.

Those screams are walled into the plaster

with yellow smoke and stale air.

They elongate the shadows with their motionless faces.

They speak to the wind

with voices of the wind caught empty

and etched in glass.

Tomorrow's moon never comes,

murdered under the leaves like a child.

The shifting base of the earth

mumbles with a voice heavy as lead,

that is so soft that it eludes my ears.

To sing a song of leeches,

who wander under the nuptial poison of bones

pleading with the crazy yearning

that possesses a night sky.

I call out with my mouth full of locust,

this brain disease of naked nymphs.

Each of them, like me,

like all those whose faces

slid along the razor's edge,

who in death have had their smiles

cut into little squares

and distributed into the bloodspattered sky.

There is no terrible remorse

sewn to the folds of my pajamas.

Even as the sleepers that awake in their flesh,

brood under the iron sky to beat at their faces.

The underground chasm,

in darkness is plunged like a glove

into the wet soil of the human voice.

The worms that bury themselves in an eternity,

they too know that they themselves,

like all the bones, must wait for their reflections.

My burial is beneath the storm

with rain raging in my ears.

The fog that consumes my tongue

like envelopes of skin,

speaks with a distant thunder.

A storm of bulls with black hair,

their wanting grins

are sheets of white under shirts

that lay across dead thighs.

The summer thunder is where the railroad ends

upon the scented lips of the poisoned dawn.

This season of the wicked is tented in crepe

and rolled in broken glass.

It seeks an entrance through the promenades of sleep.

It is sleep that wipes

its invisible hand across a night sky.

The calloused fish scale aroma of the night

is haunted with headless children.

The blooming of flowers,

like the thunder-heads of fish

are violent in their repose

and salient in their quietude.

They extend their coughing lungs

beyond the frail premise of their armor.

The naked dust that tomorrow brings

upon its horned head,

is the glowing dust that coughs ruby

and stains the ears of time.

Dust is wearing a death's head mask!

The open hole where thought escapes with a whisper,

throws itself against a wall

and lies with its feet sewn

to the garments of laughter.

Buried deep within the storm,

the swallow's throat floats

within its severed brain.

All that seems to be is beneath the wave

like the storm of shoes

and the rain of sleeping hands.

What follows the face

to the other end of oblique silence,

extends itself like a grand balloon

to expose underneath the water's edge

like a hollow bone of a jackal's jaw.

My burial of stone,

this passion held within the mackerel's belly

is like a screaming sun that resembles a dog's tooth.

My burial that is covered in spit

and the lovely flame of death,

that tames the notion of grand illusions

are cast in the wolf's eye.

Illusions, a sea of beards,

beards of snow,

a blanket of sorrow.

Illusions, illusions!

This is my breast that speaks

with a voice of a woman

caught in the clinch of devastation.

It is the wild wind that croons like a vulture.

This is my breast that speaks

the voice of tomorrow,

caught and chained like a vulture.

This is my breast, my breast of storms.

The sea has ended!

Its reflection can be seen on the ends of my lips.

The tide of urchins with wristwatches

are waiting for romance.

The delirious fluxation of an ocean

that no longer remembers.

How many anemones are murdered and raped

lying against the limit of motion?

Perhaps it's a freighter of umbrellas

unable to stop the rain.

The tears that fall

from the cheeks of a woman's heart

are so full of sails and spider web threads,

that like a glass of wine balanced on a pubic hair,

the bottoms of my feet with the dry skin of swans

are wearing saddles incrusted with swine.

Bonafide man is rising like a flame.

The phoenix of crass derangement

is dancing on yellow parchment

or is concealed in the hereditary myth of war.

Pontifical man,

with his liver of golden marsupial shadows.

The extent of the drama is drawn across a landscape

whose barren face is folded in flame.

Conical man,

with a mustache of dying autos

and graveyards sewn to the underside of his eyelashes

is playing with a deck of cards

and breaking host across tortured lips.

Even the birds with their leaf-covered heads,

their songs of solace, tunes that make swans tremble,

even they feel the heat of the incantation.

The mountain's rage is consumed

in the mounting tremolo of a horn,

like the blast that masks an aviary called chance.

Firestorms lick at my eyes.

The larynx of its embers are molded

to the bottoms of my feet,

feet already calloused with the membranes of daylight.

Swollen bloodlines,

like the necks of horses,

are placed upon a cart with clowns

dressed in cellophane.

Laughter is outlawed or nailed to the moon

where the elephant winter

intercedes with the dawn.

The holographic fever

that plays upon a xylophone of teeth,

knows no power than its own.

Babylon with its graying hair

sits high upon the beach red prattle

of the moon in despair.

The conch with a voice in full bloom

is leaving shattered!

The moisture of salt clung to the inner chambers

of a pathological winter is the dawn

with its leaves of smoke,

taking me to the river's edge

to drown my eyes in the filmy silence

That is laid upon the evening's desire.

The outgrowth of an ice age,

played out within the individual dramas

that is locked in frozen water

of baroque antiquities.

Those wooly mastodons

who enjoy the pleasure of their aloneness

are sacks of coal hung on the ears of diplomats.

Magnificent pachyderms with their hemophiliac futures

and the pallor of wet chalk

pasted to their eyelids' words that are somnambulistic,

caustic and rude.

With frozen tundra attached to their necks,

nailed into position with fingerprints,

they are waltzing in the grey mist

that shadows find in their weeping soliloquies.

Storm of hacked wings,

the river is stapled to hallucination

like a sacrifice made easy under a delirious moon.

The spectators in formal necktie

are attending the haunted banquet,

where fools dine with all the corpora,

This is the dawn

that awaits the daylight's striking blow.

My dawn filled with bile and blood.

This is the dawn of the third morning

that reeks of flesh.

This is the hour of the wolves' howl.

This is the third morning

scented in death,

when all the eyes look to the east

to see a morning that will never be.

POLITICIANS OF THE DEPRAVED

Motion sickness is necessitated by the flow of hair that is the under balance of clouds. Too many voices call out in the rain to be constituted as a replenishment of dead saints. Who stands at the apex of the day wearing the clothing of the dead; who in their despair departs on woeful wooden boats to seek the silent rose petals of the silent? So silent is their breath that they may be mistaken for the dead. So loud are their tremors of doubt that their ears are pinned to the floor. Here in the stale mists of ammonia, a woman whose hair is lit on fire by frail exasperated monks takes repose in the heat of the day by examining her own forehead with forceps made of glass. She opens a small cavity in the flesh, revealing a colony of spiders that eat at her brain causing a frontal lobotomy that leaves her transfixed in a state of agitation. It is in this state of agitation that she speaks in mumbled tones and caustic automatic phrases: "The somnambulant fish, the veiled interruption of shadows follows me to the edge of the well." She grins at the walls with no response. She pulls at her eyelids, lifting them to release a flock of birds. "Too many," she responds with a despondent glance. "There are far too many to hold on my tongue." She turns toward the door as if to leave, but her skirt is caught by the light, preventing her from any kind of movement.

Outside on the pavement a crowd gathers to elicit the crowning of the weather. Storms gather around their feet in small eddies. These pools of climatic conditions whirl about like crows. The disturbance discolors all the chaotic visitations of meteorological transmutations. The crowd shouts wordless obscenities that are frozen to their palates like thin wafers of dead skin. Policemen gather around them and peer into blocks of distortion glass that reflect the seasons of their latent brutality. It is under the guise of this reflection that they began to dislocate the tiny nerve endings of their cranial cortex.

The woman stares out her window at the crowd gathered below. A deep sorrow overtakes her and throws her into a deeper melancholia than she had ever experienced. She began to cry, but the tears were hard droplets of glass that fell to the floor, shattering, leaving tiny shards of pointed glass that gathered at her bare feet. As she paced back and forth by the window the glass cut into her flesh leaving behind a trail of blood. Her nervous condition prevented her from feeling the small cuts left by the glass and only agitated her sense of despair. "If I cry out," she thought, "they will discover that I exist, and they will come for me, and if they come for me, they might uncover my chaste and lonely solitude." She placed her hands against the panes of glass, wishing she could push away the intrusion. "If my solitary self-imposed imprisonment is discovered then they may seek to liberate me from my exile and seek to force me to reenter the world of their prying eyes. My shame would be extracted by a flock of birds and dropped like seeds into soil that is moribund and evil; the result would be the growth of weeds that would engulf the earth, with the despair that is my own."

The crowd began to grow; filling the street with upturned faces, salient whispers, shouts and cries. Their faces revealed a certain degree of futility and anxiety that exposed the temperament of mob madness. They began to stomp their feet in a cadence that suggested the heated insanity that was about to lose control. The air was thick with fear and the heat of fury; all sanity was lost as they rocked back and forth, from one foot to the other. The sky began to crack, opening up a gap in the clouds that resembled a wound. The crowd cried out as the wound began to bleed, and the blood flowed down into the streets. At the height of the frenzy something dreadful began to take place, thousands of dead birds fell from the sky: finches, larks, doves and ravens, birds of every description and size. The panic that ensued fell across the crowd like a tsunami of menace and malice.

The woman in the window collapsed to her knee's weeping, her body convulsing with fever chills that swept over her, possessing her every fiber. "I am discovered, I am doomed, and the whole world is as if it were my flesh, cancerous and filthy. I have been daunted by the very life that has cursed me from birth. I should have passed into death from the womb, stillborn and lifeless like dust." She dug her fingernails into her palms, drawing blood. She licked her hands, the acidic salt taste consuming her in delirium and loathing. "If I must, I'll remove my face and implant it with another. I'll rip my soul from this dried shell of a body and fling it to the stars where it may be consumed by a black hole or left to wander as an aimless comet without a tail." She rose to her feet and peered out the window at the crowd assembled outside. The crowd had amassed into a sea of alarm. They moved about as if blinded, aimless and without meaning. Their cries reached such a vociferous pitch of earsplitting decibels that the very air began to tremble. From a low, rumbling, opprobrious call that opens oceans of monolithic dinosaur jawbones to the shrill high-pitched soprano reverberations of mucus beetles, the nervous twitch of the air created a habitual catatonic excitation. Maldolorian ossification of the senses took every ounce of strength the woman possessed. It was by sheer will alone that she stood before the window with her forehead resting on the pane, her fingers splayed on the glass like spiders, her eyes filled with the fog of a distant sorrow. "Has there ever been a time," she cried out "that I have not been the focus for such suffering?" Her head tapped the window glass. Tap, tap, tap, and tap, in a rhythmic pulse, tap, tap, and tap. "If there were a God, would he have condemned me to this wretched soulless imitation of life? If so, then his is a miserable humor. The joke of it all lacks all amusement and taste." Tap. Tap, tap and tap, her head bounced off the window glass. The glass began to shudder as her head reverberated off the thin pane.

The glass gave way with an explosion, raining shards of razor sharp glass onto the crowd below. The glass fell; cutting through flesh, tendon and bone. Their cries were cut off as the cries escaped their mouths, falling to the ground like a cold whimper. The woman above waved her arms in the air as the crowd fell to their knees. She howled out in the blood-stained night, "EVIL, reverse the letters and it is live. To live is to be drowned in the excesses of evil." She looked down on the carnage below and shouted, "All of you, the dead who think you live, you are the face of evil, the mirror of darkness and the skin of the earth! Your souls are eaten by demons that resemble yourselves! Do you recognize them? Do they greet you in the morning when you shave or brush your teeth? This bastard universe that spawned the vile stench of murderers, rapist and child molesters, you are all politicians of the depraved!"

SPAIN CAME TOO LATE TO CAPITULATE THEIR DESIRE

I can remember my mother standing on a large silver table, smirking at the open window and undressing in the frost. Her nostrils split open, and birds made their nests in them, if only to lay the eggs of lizards. I smiled weakly from beneath the silver table that resembled ice and counted the goose bumps on my back. A shadow came through the closet, lurking across my neck and splitting it open with a waffle iron. I cried, and my tears were made of cheese that smelled of my dead grandmother's lips. Her coffin was filled with devils trumpet root and huck vine to ward off demons in leather boots.

My mother menstruated in my grandmother's hand; Grandmother thought it unspeakable in her sexual reality of smoke. Undespairingly, mother bled froth from her vigina and filled the holes in my grandmother's eyes. Suicide spoke in a voice of omnipresence and secret frustration of the owls stuck in a vase like a bouquet of deathly flowers.

Spain came too late to capitulate their desire. Beneath their rose beds, the second half of their bodies wept while sitting on soft down pillows. I breathed beneath my hiding place as quietly as the situation would allow, so as not to be discovered spying on their maniac mutations. My hand slipped to my eyes to rediscover if they were still there. The joints of my fingers ached and were swollen from pulling the wings off tiny golden spiders that often slept above my eyelids. Spain came too late; I have said that before for no apparent reason, but to capitulate their desire. Spain came too late, but I knew the fountains of Madrid, with their bullet holes, and fine marble twisted about my ankles as fine etched engravings on the walls of the nursery.

Fetishes of monkey fur and bone hung from my legs, tied there with cords of fish entrails, which had dried and cut off the circulation to my feet, which were wrapped in shrouds. I coughed and gave away my presence, which startled my mother and grandmother. They looked beneath the table and saw me shivering convulsively. This made them laugh from their nostrils, which bled images of the rosary down their cheeks. I wanted to run, but the fetishes held me fast. I only winked at them as fast as I could until they became distorted, flashing projections of an old movie. They pulled at the monkey fur, and I could feel it stinging as if it were my own hair was being yanked.

The blood of Guernica is as salty as the sea, whose feet run jumbled through the streets of my youth. Desire pinched me with long pointed poisons of nervousness. The lake in which I had drowned once ran through my mouth seeking to wet the feet of my ancestors. Spain came too late, the morning of the locus, like corpuscles dribbling from the sky. My neck felt the strain to see if my birth were approved of. Two hunters stalked through the room. They were very familiar and the game they tracked I saw in a photograph once; it was the same picture I see when I brush my teeth.

My mother came close to the table and gave me an unconcealed glance that fell from her mouth like thunder. My grandmother approached from the other side, a long electric cord trailing behind her. I could not run, but the fetishes barked. The bare wire was attached to the lobes of my head by my grandmother, who then plugged it in. As I shook on the floor, my mother wrote with her menstrual blood upon my chest: "Spain came too late to capitulate their desire."

A LITTLE STORY OF A PUPPY

The closet was full of nuns with ancient crucifixes nestled between their legs, and they cried out in the night of passions unleashed. Warm bellies carved into fortresses because apple skins are ripened on the fruit. Nuns in the closet, darkness haunting their breasts. A cold frost squeezed into the palms of their hands. A blade of sorrowful wrenching came from their lips like the cry of dogs committing lustrous acts upon their ancestors. Dried on dry racks, little balls of shit are formed into statuettes of the holy virgin mother. One of the nuns, in the tightest of leather stockings, stroked the little statuette, exclaiming as she did so, "Ohhhh! Mother Mary lead us unto salvation with your lustful smile and your skirts of iron." At this point the door of the closet swung open, and the mother superior gazed down upon the nuns with a fiery eye.

"And what is this?" she yelled.

"Please don't beat us," the nuns giggled, "with your leather whip." They panted as they squirmed. "Oh, please mother superior, not the leather tong tied about your waist."

The mother superior glared at them like fish. "So, my little nuns find pleasure amongst the shoes and balls of shit," she said. "So, my little nuns..." She repeated it over and over. The mother superior raised her habit to her waist, revealing her sex like a furry little animal. The nuns, still in the closet, stared and giggled. Mother superior put her finger deep into her vagina, pulling out a revolver. The mother superior then shot the nuns in the closet. The nuns lay on the floor bleeding, their mouths hanging open, their tongues protruding obscenely. Tattooed on the tongue of each nun were a "Hail Mary" and an "Our Father," except for the nun with the tightest of leather stockings. On her tongue was an image of God as a dog, a Great Dane, because his wind was short. He had large haunches and a massive erect ear. The mother superior glanced horrified at the wet tongue and the picture of her master the dog and she began to pant furiously. The more she panted, the wetter the revolver became. The revolver pulsed and became a potato that was rotten and full of worms. The mother superior sighed and dropped the rotten potato, which ran off across the dead thighs of the nuns.

There was a barking in the hallway. The mother superior thought that God had come to bless her. She hurried out of the room to get a glance at this great deity that since childhood haunted her each time she passed the bathroom or entered the garden to eat the roses. The barking grew louder and her excitement grew as she entered the hallway on her quest for God the dog. She looked both ways in the hallway, but saw nothing but a picture on the wall. Could it be that her lifelong quest was at an end? That God the dog was on her wall? The mother superior went to the picture that was barking. The picture was not God the dog, but a photo of the Pope, who was laughing and barking at the same time. The mother superior felt much sadness because the Pope had fooled her. There was no God the dog, only the Pope who could bark. The mother superior removed the Pope from the wall and placed him on the floor. The mother superior pissed on the Pope and the Pope excommunicated her immediately.

THE BOTTLE

Sitting where the sea cranes its neck to glimpse the horizon, a dozen pipers line themselves like mourners waiting for the procession of the dead. Their weeping awaits the oncoming footsteps of a man, me, a wanderer caught in the delusion that the sands move aside in the rustle of footfalls. It is my destiny, my gallant future caught in the wild winds of unrest. My heart pounds with the remorse bred from the knowledge of what has come to pass. This is my shivering skin covered with molten ash of that knowledge. My story is written in the grains of sand, written in the blood-red stains of knowing.

I remember the wind like the rustle of old bones. It came from the distance like a haunting whisper. The wind moved with the smoothness of a woman's voice. It lay upon my shoulder, draped like a smoldering flag. I remember the hour, the moment and the exact degree of the moon in the sky. I writhe in the agony of the knowledge. The knowledge of what has come to pass and the knowledge of what is yet to transpire. It is much like a clock with no hands, with no numbers, and with no sound to mark time's passing. The past marks the future as the same moment. It is a delusion of a haunted dream in a mirror that has been painted black.

My name is of no importance. I am as I have always been through the eons, a wisp of mist caught within the folds of time. I turn to the moon and see my face implanted there. To tear down the walls of screams that had been constructed before me, the story must be told. I wish to find a listener, one with ears that are brave enough to bear the weight. Now that I have your attention, I shall not let you go until the seas have unburdened their shoulders, and I tell my tale of wonderment.

Through the spice-filled streets I roamed, looking for the future in a glass bottle. It seems that my eyes have wandered forever amongst the smoke-filled containers of a thousand bazaars. One bottle, a bottle as red as blood on a moonless night and as dark as an empty soul, to find it, I have traveled the globe. I have sought it out in my dreams and I have seen it lingering on the edges of reality with its hideous shapes, suggesting some wildly erotic phantasmagoria. The subtle curvature of line and light gives it the hallucinatory impression that it is alive. Seeing the bottle in my dreams fills me with a haunting desire to obtain this apparition, even as it fills me with loathing.

In Cairo I was led to a small tent just at the outskirts of the city. I was lead there by a blind boy who dragged a dead guide dog. He led me to a tent as black as ebony. From the doorway there bled a snake of amber light and a scent of ancient pleasures. The boy bid me to be seated and disappeared out of the opening. Looking about the tent, I observed that it was devoid of any furnishings except for two pillows and a small table between them. Upon the table was a box so beautifully inlaid that it drew my fingers to touch. The box lid was fastened with a small gold pin. Carefully removing the pin, I opened the box. At the bottom of the box lay a calling card made of the finest filigree of spider web and sewn to that as with the most delicate of care was the inscription:

Thruurn Del Cotisis
*Seller * Collector*
Of Fine & Exotic Receptacles

I raised my head, and sitting before me was a small and rather portly man who wore a grin that creased his face in a most devilish manner. I started to speak, but he cut me off with the raising of one of his chubby fingers. "There is no need for introductions," he said. "I have been following your progress for some time. In fact, you have become quite an object of curiosity to me. I have found your search somewhat amusing."

"You know of the bottle?" I asked.

"Know of the bottle?" he replied with a laugh. "You'll have to excuse me if I seem to find humor in your question. I do indeed know of the bottle. I am its owner!"

I stared across at Thruurn Del Cortisis, his grin was unchanging, his manner unsettling. Behind his grin I could feel that a deep sorrow lingered, a sorrow so deep that its scars cannot be masked by the mask of a grin. Silence lingered in the air like a heavy veil. When at last Del Cortisis spoke, his smile fell from his face like melting wax. "Your search for the bottle has not only brought me curious amusement, but a great deal of agitation and fear. The bottle, as you know, is very old. Its history is known only by those whose scholarly pursuits turn toward the most esoteric matters. Its history is veiled in mystery, violence and death. Your own curiosity and unflinching pursuit may well have plunged us both headlong into blackness as deep as the soul and more terrible then the trenches of hell."

I felt flushed in the face, and words were thick like a paste in my mouth. "I know little of the bottle's history, only that it is rare, and it is said to have value beyond measure."

"Rare is not the word, my friend," he said with his grin returning to his face. "It is the only one of its kind. Its value can only be measured by its presence in history."

"And its history?" I inquired.

"Oh yes, its history," he mused. "If you please, let us make ourselves comfortable." With that he spread his hands, and within the instant that it takes to blink the eye, he produced a bottle of wine and two silver cups. As he poured the liqueur, he gave me a wink. "Magic in one of the benefits of age…"

"Before the dawn of man, when the dust still swirled in the mythological ethers, there existed something that was neither man nor beast. It spent its time at an inner wickedness, playing a game of self-torture and degradation. It fouled the air and the seas. It laid waste across the earth till the lands' barren breast split and coughed up the blood-red film from the very bowels of its core. It lay in its filth for a millennium, gorging itself and growing fat. The dust of the ages began to weave a deeper torment into its soulless existence. It became bored. It waited! It waited in silence and in a death-like hibernation. Millennium upon millennium passed its glazed-over eyes. Storms settled in and washed clean the earth. It waited! Creatures were born and raised from the sea. It waited! Age upon age passed in unknowing ignorance, yet still it waited. Then one day it roused itself out of its slumber. Something worthy had come, something that carried the spawn of wickedness and cruelty. It walked upon two legs: It was called man.

"The dark thing awoke itself, shaking loose the dust of eons. Now it could mate. Now it could feed. Man, in ignorance, but not innocence, heard its moans and rolled into the dark moon-lit forest. The dark thing satiating itself grew in the delight of its wanton lust. Man emerged from the forest with a new light in his eye, with a hunger of his own.

"The throat was slit, and the blood flowed forth, and the dirt of the earth became as rust. The hunger of violence swung its contorted presence

forward hovering, like a shadow in the sky. Man looked to the heavens and created gods to deliver him, but deliverance was not incoming, only blood and fear-filled eyes reflected the flame of sorrow. The ravages of a cruel laughter played in the ear of human folly as blood encircled the earth. The silence that greeted the morning was now filled with the moaning of the living. That silence that once stroked the ears of the placid dawn now belonged to the domain of the dead. With the centuries came the cloak of knowledge, and it was adorned with the jewels of power. Beneath the cloak were practitioners of sorcery and the arts of necromancy and illusionism. They created gods in ravenous forms that demanded servitude or else promised devastation. In the eyes of one, the jewels had a particularly bright gleam. That caused him to think.

"He was a sorcerer; a dark moody figure that paced back and forth in front of his altar. His shadow loomed high against the wall giving him a monstrous appearance. His voice rang out in the night like a cold bell toll. "It's there," he said, looking out at the sky. "I can feel the presence of darkness, like a disease eating away at my bones. I can feel the haunting unbalance of nature. It is stronger than I, stronger than all of the false gods, stronger than the nature of the elements themselves."

"The wind howled in the distance, carrying with it a voice more terrible than the volcanic rumblings of the earth. "I am here, Wizard. The earth has moved aside for me, and I am hungry." The mouth that was not a mouth, but a gaping black hole, spoke with a voice of unending nothingness. "My hunger is insatiable. Do you know what that means?" It rasped bile and retched. "Do you know what it is to live forever in a deep unsatisfied lust? No, of course you wouldn't: You are a mortal man. Mortal men find their satisfaction only in death."

"The sorcerer turned his back upon the dark thing. "I'm not a sorcerer of ill power. I find you unsavory, to be sure. But I do not disturb as easily as you might think." He walked over to a mirror that seemed to be filled with smoke that lingered just beyond his reflection. He reached his hand through the mirror that rippled as if it were water. When he pulled his hand back, it held a small clear receptacle of glass encased in silver. Its stopper bore a figure that had a body resembling a gargoyle and a head that was fat and bloated with tentacles that wrapped around the neck of the bottle. The sorcerer gently pulled the stopper from the bottle, muttering an incantation so vile that the sky trembled and blackened

with clouds.

"The air began to swirl, the dark thing wailed and spat. Spinning in a whirlwind of smoke and mist it began to be sucked into the bottle. As the dark thing passed into the bottle, it called out with mocking words: "Have you prepared yourself for the end of time? Have you prepared for the delicate unbalance in the nature of things? I assure you that I am. I could well do without the stench of human existence. I have waited for eons, and I will wait eons more: But I assure you this: I curse on you, sorcerer. You shall not rest until the end of time. You will live to witness the devouring. You shall not age a day, but your soul will beg for release. I will wait!" The sorcerer placed the stopper into the bottle, placed it in his robe, and disappeared into the night."

Del Crotisis folded his hands and smiled. "I hope my story was entertaining," he said. "And I hope you understand the full importance of the situation." He brought from his coat lapel a small bottle of hideous design. He laid it upon the table. "I was quite prepared. I see a look of surprise on your face. Please don't press me for explanations. Let it be sufficient, that I, Thruurn Del Cortisis, am one and the same as that moody sorcerer of long ago. I, Thruurn Del Cortisis with my shrewdness and knowledge imprisoned that dark, nether beast within this forbidding bottle. I also fated myself to a living death, a constant doom, to a knowledge more terrible then any held by any man. I knew you would come for the bottle. The thing inside knew." He held the bottle up before me. "It has waited a long time. It waited at the gates of Troy. It waited beneath the great mounds of the dead. It waited at Waterloo, Bunker Hill and Gettysburg. It was present at the blitzkrieg and Aushwitz. It waited with patience at Jonestown. It witnessed murder and greed from the first marching armies to genocide in South Africa. I felt you coming like a terrible wind. I could not persuade you to give up your quest any more then I could keep the sun from rising at dawn. The bottle is yours, and at last I can greet my death. The dusk has come, and with it the bloody moon.

The bottle burned my hands. I felt a scream welling up in my throat. I felt my ears explode with a raspy laughter that only my ears could hear. I now possessed a bottle that cast its shadow across the earth, in turn I was possessed by an object of glass that set my nights in fear and bathed my days in darkness. Hours passed into days. My eyes reddened from sleepless nights. Madness gripped my mind as each night the bottle called to me. My nerves were strained from the endless beckoning. My resistance and reserve wore thin. My hands fondled the bottle with nervous anticipation. With a nerve splitting-scream, I opened the bottle.

Fire raged in a storm of supreme violence. A hot wind blew across the earth. Skin blistered and peeled, leaving raw flesh and bone. Where once stood living beings, now only the shadows remained. The sun was blotted out by a cloud that rose into the sky, and from the cloud came a haunting laughter as the life and soul of the earth was sucked dry.

Sitting where the sea cranes its neck to glimpse the horizon, a dozen pipers line themselves like mourners waiting for the procession of the dead. Their weeping awaits the oncoming footsteps of a man, me, a wanderer caught in the delusion that the sands move aside in the rustle of footfalls. It is my destiny, my gallant future caught in the wild winds of unrest. My heart pounds with the remorse bred from the knowledge of what has come to pass. This is my shivering skin covered with molten ash of that knowledge. My story is written in the grains of sand, written in the blood-red stains of knowing.

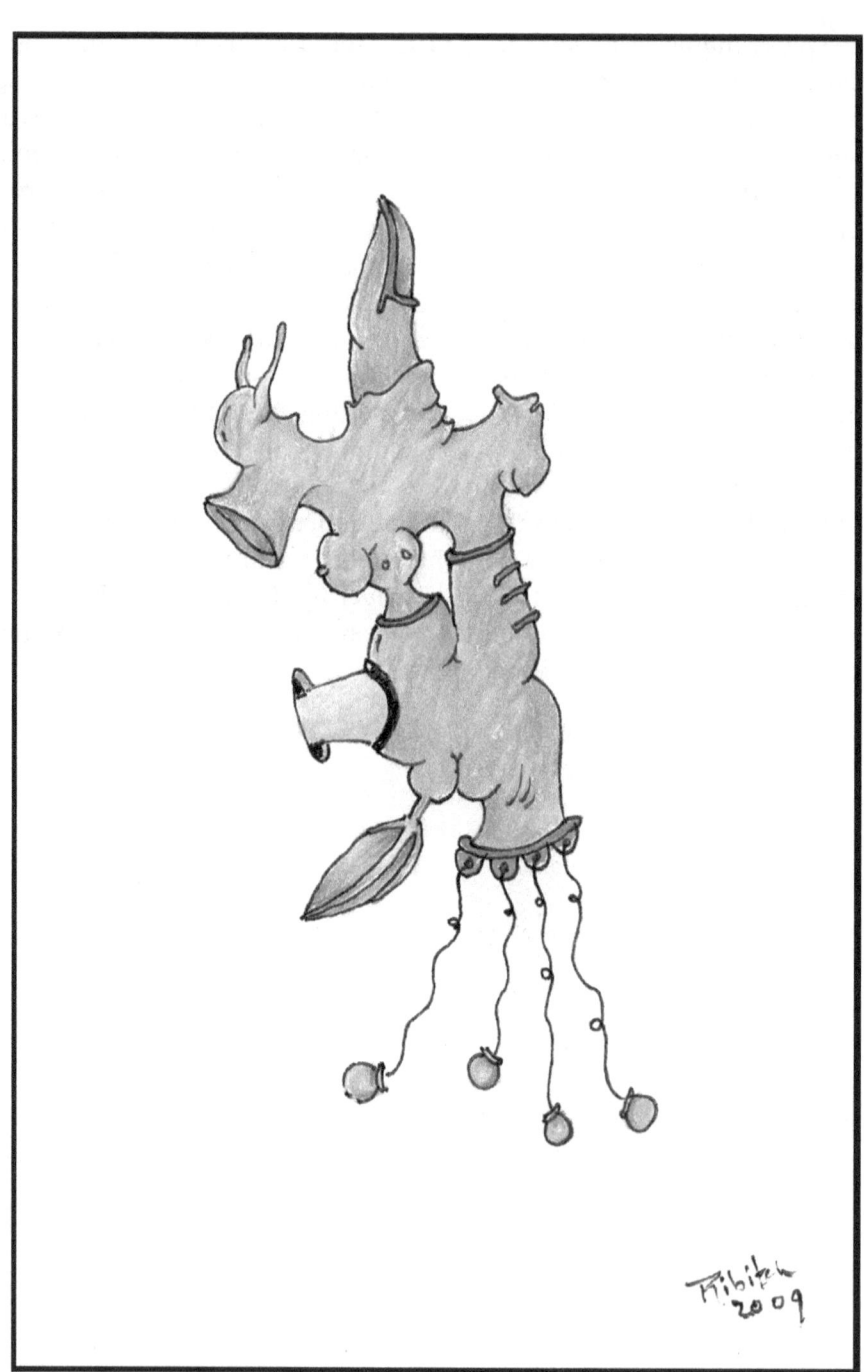

THE CORRESPONDENCE

My dear friend Wandering Jack,

There are deserts and deserts, and you are one of them... I found myself thinking of you the other day. The wind was a melancholy bystander dressed in a black coat, counting all the birds that flew by. That was when I found myself thinking of you. You have been gone such a long time. I think that you have perished. How does it feel to be in death? You have wandered far from the life, as we knew it... Your mother came by! What could I tell her, what could I say? There are statues erected in your honor. They are cracked and worn. Perhaps the day of your return will come, your resurrection. I have waited for thirty years now; my beard has grown to such lengths that I sleep under it as though it were a blanket. Speaking of sleep, I dreamt of you yesterday. In my dream you wore a frock coat covered with stalactites. You resembled the earth. You were very old. I hardly recognized you, but you spoke to me. Your voice had that familiar sound. You told me of your death beneath the wheels of a train.

What could I tell her, what could I say? Remember the time when we were young? We would watch the trains pass on the trestle and dream of long off days that trailed smoke like a winding worm. We dreamed of clouds covered in silk. You told me that you would ride the back of the worm like a cowboy. There was dust in your eye. I could see it made you cry. We were so young, but age clung to the edges of our faces like old cobwebs.

What could I tell her, what could I say? There are no more trestles, there are no more billows of smoke, there are only monorails, electrical bloodlines that connect the dead with the dead. Even the skin of the earth is blistered and is no longer brown, but a pale dead gray. They still sing your name, those who dream under the splintered remains. What could I tell her, what could I say?

(You can count on me when the whistle blows.)
Until that time...
 Mr. Bones

*   *   *

Dear Mr. Bones,

I think I miss you as well, especially that unruly mop that sits atop your head like a flaming nest of a bird. It has been a long time. The years cover my suitcase like mold, and like mold, those years are at times hard to breathe.

This dream of yours disturbs me. I find myself thinking of it often. The dust follows on my heels and I can't seem to shake it. Yes it's true that I died under the wheels of far too many trains. It's funny how you mention our youth. That was a thousand years ago, and I don't think I can remember any of it. Perhaps if I sleep, it will come back to me in dreams. Perhaps if I sleep, I will see what it is that follows me with such persistence.

Remember me in your dreams!
Your old friend Wandering Jack

P.S. Tell mother nothing, it would only create more questions.

*   *   *

Dear Wandering Jack,

Nothing seems the same anymore, but it was good to hear from you. I can't get your smile out of my mind. It was always such a warm welcoming smile. I hope that it is still a part of your face. It would seem so empty without it. I fear that I am growing old. I can't seem to concentrate on the cards any more. I lost a fortune last week and I can't seem to recover.

Do you remember San Antonio Red? She was a rodeo star back in 1952. She showed up yesterday with some vague notion that you were still alive. Are you? Or do I correspond with a ghost, a vague notion conjured out of my failing memory.

I smelled the smoke of an old freight before I awoke this morning. I asked myself if it were a dream, but it lingered and mingled with the bitterness of my coffee. Perhaps it's that old whore, memory, again. I can feel the sharp claws of her presence lash at my throat, where every so often I feel a lump.

In tears I reply.
Friends always, Mr. Bones

*   *   *

My Dear Mr. Bones,

How it is that you go on with the past, some deep-seated memory of yours? All that I have is a cheap mirror from Woolworth's that I use to shave my face once a month. Even as I stare into its scratched surface, I can no longer recognize the face that greets me there. It's a ghost that I no longer know. He wears a grimy old Stetson hat. (May have owned it since my skin was pink and smooth with youth.) My skin is now yellow and cracked from the years and miles that coat it like graveyard dust. I see eyes that are set deep in the hollows of my skull. It is a lifeless cave where no fires burn.

San Antonio Rose? No, I don't want to remember. Tell them I am dead. Keep alive only the myth of my death. I only keep my correspondence with you because we were born in the same hellish wind. We took our first breath from the same dust of despair. We are the same, you and I, as if we were cast from the same seed. I guess that too is memory. It is a wound full of pus.

My dirge was the last freight whistle out of Kansas City. Don't wait up too long for me! A man can lose a lot of sleep.

I remain your friend.
Wandering Jack

*   *   *

105

Dear Wandering Jack,

You are so far away and the whistle no longer blows. Where is the young cowboy sitting on the fence, his eyes full of dreams, his heart full of adventure? I saw him board a train and disappear in smoke and cinder.

I have a bag of marbles. I've separated all the claries. They resemble moons. So many moons! The bag is etched with an old wood burning set with the word: "JACK". God, these marbles are cold. They freeze my hand.

What can I say…?

Your mother was by again. I believe she is dying. I can see it in the eyes. She asks about you. She always asks. It's hard to lie in the face of someone's death.

What can I say…?

I can only avert my eyes and peer deep into a handful of moons, cold ice moons that rattle when I shake my hand like wheels on a steel rail. Before my hand freezes, I must pour these moons back into a leather bag with those big clumsy letters, "JACK"

Waiting as always,
Mr. Bones

*   *   *

My Dear friend Wandering Jack,

It's been six months since I last wrote, and nearly a year since I heard from you. Where does it all go? The time, the years? I can hear the mourning doves singing in the snow. How sad they sound, as if to mourn the coming of the sun. I can't walk any longer; my legs have shriveled up under me. The doctors say they don't know what is wrong. I know, I've always known.

Running along the rail. Wait Jack wait!

Sitting down and crying tears as big as the state of Texas. The cold steel on my rump felt like it would cut me in two. I could hear that distant rumble even then.

Running along the rail. Wait Jack wait!

I'm haunted, Jack, by a thousand memories that won't let go. They hold me like shackles to the walls of this room. I am nailed to a stack of old photos that are stained yellow with the decay of age. Old toys line my shelf like dying soldiers.

Running along the rail. Wait Jack wait!

As always
Mr. Bones

*   *   *

Dear Wandering Jack,

Your mother died this spring. Before she went she asked, "Where is Jack?"

What could I tell her, what could I say?

The morning doves sang for her. It's funny but their song resembled the distant whistle of a train blanketed in fog. I was the only one present at her funeral. I buried with her a bag of moons bearing the name "JACK".

What could I tell her, what could I say?

With all respects
Mr. Bones

*   *   *

My Dear friend Mr. Bones,

What prisons we make for ourselves. I've been behind bars many times in all these years, but none so binding as those upon the heart. You with your memories, old photographs, forgotten toys and marbles that are moons. And me with my shoes full of holes, my eyes full of smoke and my head full of dreams that run along the rail faster than I can run. My arms are outstretched, grasping only the ghost of my desire. It eludes me like a chimera veiled in the soft down of spider webs.

I chased it through the flatlands of the American dream, letting it slip through my fingers. I followed it to Mexico and into the steaming jungles of South America. I chased it across the ocean and hunted it in the alleys of Paris. I climbed the highest peaks of the Himalayas hoping to trap it in the rock crags and snowy depths. It took me to the orient and it eluded me in its smells and exotic tapestries. It lead and I followed, or at least that is what I thought.

Now it is clear to me that I did not pursue it, but it pursued me. It chased me like a hound of hell across the earth. I ran to keep ahead of it, not to follow it. I glanced over my shoulder only to see its nostrils flared and its teeth bared in hot pursuit.

Going back to an old letter of yours, in which you said, "There are deserts and deserts and I am one of them." I have sought after water without seeing the sea. I have searched for flowers, not noticing that they grew up from my toes. Even with this knowledge, I hear the whistle moan and my feet began to run. I desire to ride the back of the worm like a cowboy; to ride it into eternity.

You will have to excuse me now; there is dust in my eye.

> Till the whistle brings me home
> I remain your friend always,
> Wandering Jack

*   *   *

Dear Wandering Jack,

Running along the rail. Wait Jack wait!
Running along the rail. Wait, Jack wait!

Mr. Bones

*   *   *

Dear Sir:

I am sorry to inform you of the death of Mr. Jack Thomson. The cause of death was an apparent suicide. Since Mr. Thomson has no living relatives, we are mailing you his possessions. Enclosed, you will find one mirror, a Stetson hat and box of correspondence. His body shall be shipped by rail, as he instructed.

Regretfully yours
J. Allen Carter
Coroner
Amarillo, Texas

*   *   *

Dear Wandering Jack,

Running along the rail. Wait, Jack Wait!

Mr. Bones

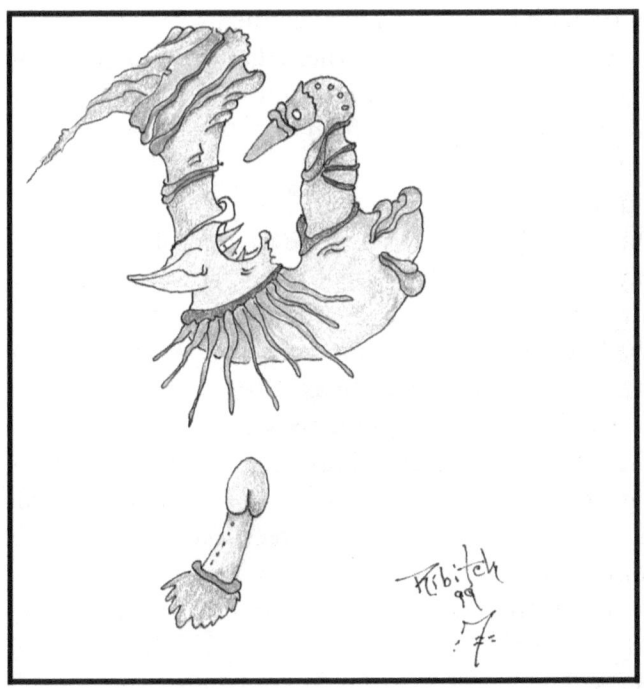

DELTA BLUES

Black cat bone across my collar like a 44 long barrel
That reaches down my side like a stiff erection
Delta screams, the moan of the Delta down
The crossroads where 61 and 49 meet upon the hips of the dead
Their backs are bent with the blues
The blues with its swivel haunches of a mad dog
Blood on the tracks and on the eyelids of the catfish bottoms
Crossing the Yellow Dog exciting a fever of the oncoming Peavine
Muddy footprints across the highway
The crossroads, where at midnight the moon sings harmony on a perch
The bones of fallen guitar players who have slept beneath the moon
Waiting for the devil to tune their guitars
A whole host of finger-picking skeleton horses
Who play the Georgia skin game on the back of a black snake bone?
Delta heartbeat, the deep down of black mud
King Cotton with his smile of hanged men
Who swing from shadow trees where the Mississippi moon
Hides amongst the cattails and mosquito moss
The plow stands rusting in the field
Like an old corpse
The Delta smells of blood and mud
The Delta smells of the blues and the rhythm of slavery
The Delta cries out with the tears of the black mud
And death whistles in the graveyard of the hateful
Where the human voice of a slide guitar wails like a dead man.
The Delta with scars across its back
The open wounds of whips and rope
Where the penitentiary gate swings shut on forced labor
And King Cotton with bristled breast crows across the river
Mojo bags are hung from magnolia trees like dew drops
Hung from a Mississippi moon
Harmonica's moan broke and hungry, ragged and dirty
The hoodoo woman has left her door open till the flood waters recede
When she will gather up the mud in her hands

To form little figures of saints and husbands, pickers and ramrods
The Delta with its skin colored in the blues
Whiskey brown and Mississippi mud black
White cotton stained red with blood
The rising flood waters cannot wash it away
But can bury it deep in the rich bottom land soil
From West Memphis to New Orleans
The sound of the jook and the rollicking barrelhouse
The sound of the night wringing its hands of the day
The sound of the mule dying in the sun
It is carried by the whistle of the B & O
On the steel veins of the Southern
Or the watery backbone of a river that holds the secrets
Of the Delta, whose flesh, is our flesh,
Whose tears are our tears sewn to our cuffs not to be forgotten
These blues, like a steel guitar, ring in the night
Sounding the voice of the Delta
Like a scream in the American fabric
The Delta carries its pride along with its shame
Inside a battered guitar case
That is thrown across the shoulders of a bluesman
Who has wandered from the root
And the waters of his birth...
The Delta.

THE FLATTERIST

The Flatterist solemnly addressed himself to a large white door. He bowed and broke the latch, which caused a terrible rumbling and an emotional state. The door swung open revealing a tundra of moss that smelled of a fragrance of fur when it is wet. A wind caught the lining of a curtain and blew it far to the other corner of the room. The Flatterist entered the room and kneeled at a set of feet. The room was filled with the corpora of policemen. The Flatterist went to the window and opened it to let out a flock of birds that carried away the policemen's caps. The Flatterist smiled, but these teeth were faces cut from a magazine. The corpora of the policemen lay inert, but a strange music escaped from their eyes. A man in a white suit came out of a vestibule riding a bicycle. He rode past the Flatterist and removed a portion of his scalp. The Flatterist sat in a chair made of wire. He held an iron skillet full of fish. The fish flopped about in the throes of suffocation. A woman who wore a white hospital gown came out of a dresser of gossamer spiderwebs. She carried a camera and took a picture of the Flatterist. It took sixty minutes for him to get his picture; during that time he ate his gloves. The woman gave him the photograph and returned to her chamber of shimmering. The Flatterist looked at his photograph; it was a portrait of his dead father. His father's beard was full of maggots, and the Flatterist slapped at them, beating his father mercilessly till his hands were soaked in blood. The Flatterist wept when he read the headlines of the newspaper.

"OLD MAN FOUND DEAD, BEATEN TO DEATH BY AN UNKNOWN ASSAILANT; THE OLD MAN WAS A POLICEMAN."

The Flatterist gazed around the room; the corpora were replaced with player pianos. At each piano sat a dwarf in silence. The Flatterist cried out, but his voice was only steam. One dwarf got up from the piano and went to the window, where he leaped out. One by one, the remaining dwarfs followed the example of the first.

The Flatterist opened an envelope marked for him. The envelope was empty. The Flatterist began to weep; he wept so uncontrollably that his body began to tremble. His clothes began to rot away from his body. When the Flatterist was completely naked, and still trembling from emotional fever, he went to the closet and opened it. The closet was full of policeman's uniforms. He put one on. It was caked with blood and smelled of his father's cigar smoke. The Flatterist entered another room where he heard a woman weeping. The woman, who was naked, was sitting beside a coffin and weeping feverishly. The Flatterist walked over to the woman. The woman was his mother. The coffin was empty. The Flatterist entered the coffin and looked up into his mother's eyes that were not eyes, but large black beetles. The Flatterist had an erection that seemed confined within the policeman's trousers. The mother lay down on top of the Flatterist, but instead of being a woman, she became an insect that was disgusting. The Flatterist vomited bile of leaves. The mother insect sucked blood from his chest until she was fat and bloated from feeding.

A barking was heard from inside the Flatterist's pants; the Flatterist was possessed with fear as the barking grew louder. A dogcatcher came into the room on a complaint and pulled at the Flatterist's zipper. A Doberman pincher bound out of the trousers and attacked the dogcatcher, ripping him to a bloody mess. The Flatterist looked at the remains and discovered it was his father.

The disgusting insect was not ignored. Because its wings were made of glass mirrors, the Flatterist could see himself very clearly. He knew each line in his face as they had been avenues of emotion and canals of his fear. The disgusting insect turned on itself and ate the wings of mirrors, so the Flatterist could not see the resemblance between himself and his father.

Thirty years passed by and the Flatterist died at the same age as his father. He was buried in a room full of policemen. His father came to the funeral as a child, as his son. That's the way it was and that's the way it has always been.

VISIONS OF LOVE IN A VIOLENT SEA

The mist of languid vision swims in the sea
near a madman, drunk and delirious.
His language like blood whispered the dreams of storms,
like a delicate shadow of sleep.
I moan with the moon, but she drools on my tongue.
I sit under her white dress of winter,
watching her luscious honey forest.
I lick the rose of skin she worships
and in my lust I play with beauty as if it will crush me.
We recall our frantic moments at a sordid life,
only after love and death have cooled.
Eternity screams, but I am flooded in a black void,
like a chain trembling with violent pleasure.
I stroke the hair of silhouettes, who kiss a throbbing ecstasy,
drunk of the miasma of the dead, who convulse like my cock.
I approach a nude body that is glistening between her sex of glass.
She murmurs beneath a thousand pubic hairs.
Blue and perfect she rusts like an exquisite knife,
her mouth whispers a fierce drug;
beauty delicious and sweet.
Bare are her breasts and mad is my urge to swallow them.

THE SLEEPING CHAMBER

In honor of a dream on the pediment of a funeral veil, ill omen sobbed on the verge of personal reflections. It danced on the crest of phantoms, in the shade of closed eyelids. It falls to the earth where seas of smoke wait, spread out like a blanket. Lubricious fish haunt the avenues, pulling the carts of their dreams down slopes, whilst the men cease work to bring up the skin of their faces. Later, towards midday, I discover a swaying devil fish. The sand left to his sleep, no longer compelled to sift the hair of seaweed through the sorrows of slumber.

It is my intention to wade into deeper waters. There is something that cries out from the shadows like the continuous hum of the newborn Sybil. The ocean dances, drowning distant shipwrecks beyond the horizon of gaslight and iron. Eyelids torture the pavement for the nudity of its skin. The flesh, luminous, listening, interprets the evening storms in drunken mutilation, approaching exhausted glacial destiny without spectral warning.

The homunculus evening gown of the dawn, worn like a flounce collar, draped on the icy white shoulders of the dead. Seeing a dream that peels itself from a pillow like old paint. The blanket those odd times reveal puzzling the runestones, copper masks, razor eyelids and ancient rooms that house the mirrored floors.

Dance of the narrow shade, whose salt block throbs under those esthetes of city skin. Snow without insolent leather exploring the sidewalk in jackets of feathers, the fashion of serpents. Night opened a marvelous mirror, transparent as a rosy shell, flaming as a red snapper and proudly satisfied as the metamorphosis of wild beast. The surface of the inviolate mahogany screams in opalescence. The corolla of water will, in time and drunkenness, cut the milky passions that make a stand on the coastal plains. There they will persuade children whose hands surely will not hesitate to shadow the lighthouse, or consecrate the scarcity of memory. The moon comes and goes with the tide along the narrow path obscured by briars and hair. The voices that are tethered to the darkness fuse the garden to the woman's shoulders. The felony of glow worms tortures the earth with cocobolo wood, claws so hard as to spill forth across the earth in a giant gust.

The souvenir fetish of bone and buffalo had nickels hanging from the waist of a cemetery stature of the virgin who stands half in the shadow, whispering to the dead and the hummingbirds that dip their pearl eyes in the salt marshes of the dew. No longer still, the face of the bride turns from the dog that faithfully waits for his master's return like a star hung in the heavens for centuries until the wind comes and blows the dust of bones in a scurry across neglected lawns.

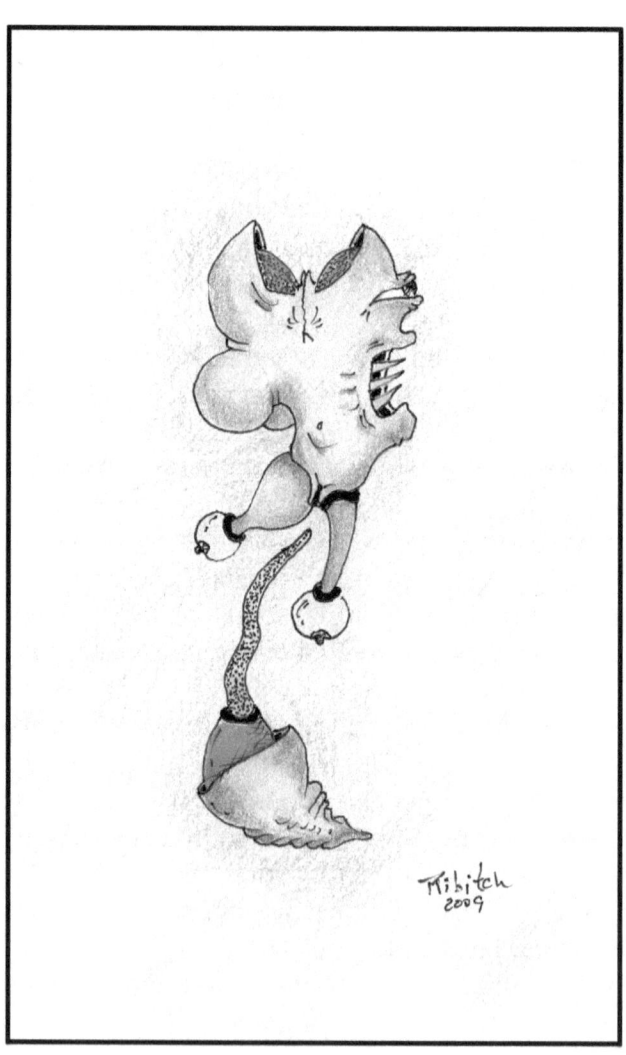

DEAR ELEVATOR SHOE

Time sure has flown! Sometime in the night a rending crash awakened me. I knew the frost demons had come. All of their confessions seeped under the door like sticky goo. I'm sure you would have raged, as those silly confessions have always angered you. I hope that they won't linger long. They always leave such a mess.

When are you returning? It's been so long, that the years seem like an old blanket that waves in the wind. When you return, I will take you to the zoo to see the cringing peccaries. They have been waiting for your return with an eager lust. Their cage has been redecorated with verbena leaves to induce sleep and promote dreams. You would be pleased with their development. They no longer are of substance, but of shadow and light. Sometimes when I visit them, their dreams seem to invade my own brain like peeping toms. Once the dream was so powerful, that it clung to the edges of my eyelids for three days. When are you returning?

The seams of my jacket have fallen apart. I have hung it upon the wall as a shrine. I place a fresh rose in the lapel every day in ritual praise to the whiteness of your teeth. The walls are yellow now. The cracks are like rivers edging the way to the sea. My eyes cannot escape the staring monotony of the glaring jaundiced interior.

I'll see you under my eyelids,

Your friend Gummo, who is dead.

DREAM OF GLASS GLOVES

A dream of glass gloves
Hung above the counter like a bird.
Behind them a woman's dark face
Clouded within the mysterious cloud of translucence.
A dream of glass gloves,
Whose fingers protrude like razors.
Shreds of paper-thin flesh,
Cut into morbid masks,
Cut into silhouette dolls,
Cut into crescent moons and stars.
A dream of glass gloves
Or the orificial offering of their light
Seen through an apparent moon.
The laughing soliloquy of disguise.
A dream of glass gloves
Filled with pale hands,
Filled with iced water,
Filled with seaweed and groupers,
Filled with no more then an ominous night.
A dream of glass gloves
That covers a laughing storm.
The sweet silent stream of reflection
Entangled in fingertips,
Like a dream of glass gloves

THE ROOM

There was a shadow, bending over the precipice of the room, that was filled with cancerous intent and eyeing all ambivalence, that brought itself up to the height of the room's ceiling. The window was open, only to the slightest degree and could not filter enough light to dissipate the warning. This is a room of smoke and shadow. This is a room of storms hung from cracked yellow plaster. The room edges itself with nervousness and laughs at the dark corners. This is my room, the only one I could know. This room is tattooed with distant relations and the fog of memory. This room!

I shift myself from one foot to the other, avoiding the clammy touch of the floor. The walls speak in whispers, then in shouts and then in monotone rhythms. The photographs on the wall are filled with insidious eyes and half-twisted smiles. They are photographs whose images are etched in wild despair. If I would burn them, their ashes would grapple with my legs and drag me down to drown in the pungent perfume of their memory. Those photographs, not framed, but stapled to the walls shift and turn their backs to me.

Each hour I spend in the room, I am unraveling the delirious webs of night that are caught within here. This is a room of tattoos. This is a room of noxious fumes and dreams. In the corner, a small boy is stapled to the wall; his grin has fallen to the floor like a withered bird. The crack that runs across his forehead is sealed in cellophane, it is also his last testament. There is a slender thread near the corner from which hangs a laughing man who swings where no breeze lingers. The sound of my breath lay upon the windowpane like cold lips of stone. Next to the boy is an old man who is caught in the act of ejaculation. Portions of his eyes have been removed. His pants are soiled with the yellowness of time. The boy and the old man are related by the attachment of their ears, their ears of rice cakes. This room of atonement is filled with the aging eyes of glaciers. The cold memories of photo albums, worn with age, like the haunting dust that is settled on the floor. A woman crosses the room across the ceiling, dragging behind her an old automobile. Her parasol is set aflame, and her eyes are set in madness. She looks about the room in a terrified manner, seeing my crumpled form in the corner.

There was a television set in the room once, but only its shadow remains. I have a photo of it over by the open window. I watch it for hours until with sadness it leaps out the window. A blood stain remains on the sill, along with some strands of string. The strings run down the wall and across the floor, where they are attached to the end of the bed. I attach my dreams to the ends of the strings at night and let them float above my bed. In the morning they are added to the photographs. They are all cracked and bleeding. One was a little dog named Puddles. A trail of urine runs down the wall and gathers on the floor beneath him. A chair is drowning there; it went down and never came up. I saw it go down. I saw it in this room of bones, in this room of flesh.

There are over a thousand photographs now. They all stare out with pig eyes and hysterical mouths. I know them all but have no idea who they are. They sleep on mats around the room and tie their dreams to the same strings as mine. In the morning there will be more of them crowding me into a corner. They live in the room. They die and are reborn in the room of laughing cracked eyes. I tried to move once, but they brought me back and chained me to the wall. The room smells like burning rodents, a putrid smell of crackling flesh. I see the twilight from my window, and it calls to me like an old lover. I have often tried to follow, but these chains bind me here. The chains are made of hornets' wings and are wrapped with delicate precision.

All the mirrors in this room are covered in black cloth, or else they are painted red. They, too, are tied with strings and attached to the end of my bed. There is no longer any resemblance between myself and the photographs that are stapled to the walls. They are photographs of my dreams, attached to my bed, attached to legs and attached to the follicles of my hair. They are photographs of a room of atonement, and a room full of crowds. The room itself is attached to a string hovering above my bed that has no room. The room is tattooed in black and white. This is a room that no one is allowed to see.

THREE SHADOWS OF THE MOON

Three shadows sat down to dinner, their elongated forms hovered above the seats like cold, dark ravens. They waited in silence, their dark featureless faces bent inward to the flickering of a single candle. The candle was set within a circle and a pentagram of pale grey ash. On the outer, cardinal points of the circle lay four stones. To the north, a blood-red stone that pulsed like a minute heart. To the west, a blue stone, that appeared to be wet or full of some mucus liquid. To the south, a white stone, luminescent as the full of the moon. To the east, an opaque colorless stone that resembled a baby's breath.

The table shivered like a cold bleak wind. The shadows sat within their silence. The room is filled with smoke and spiderwebs that sink into the dream mire of silent fog. Laughter fills the room like a haunting wave, grabbing at the legs of the shadows. One of the shadows stood, in oblique silence her arms extend like a flickering spray. Her fingers spread, enveloping the room with ghost like acquiescence. Her voice was a tremor of wind, softly filling the room.

> "Moon of spiders,
> a woman's heart of triangles' dances;
> the night seeks the illusory luminescence.
> We three shadows of the moon,
> Our heart of hearts,
> Our timely hours
> And the fleeting somnambulant mood
> Of we three shadows."

The shadow shifted her weightlessness in the room. A slight hum accompanied her, like the fire-swift fluttering of egret's wings. Her laughter personified the shifting repose of the silk black curtains.

The second shadow stood, her form twirling around the room. Her long seaweed-like hair was making sonorous tones as she turned. She spun faster and faster, till there was nothing but a blur. She hovered above the table, her rotation slowing but never halting. She sang out, her voice was more a whistle clinging to the air.

"We three shadows of the moon,
   walking in the hierophant twilight.
   The coffin beds of our hour,
   A needle is threaded with hair,
   The black oval of our shoulders,
   walking in the breast of the moon.
   We three shadows of the moon,
   tie to our sex, the thread of silence."

She slowly rotated to the corner of the room, where she melded with the flat of the wall. The darkness of her eyes remained stationary above the table. The third shadow, with a quivering nervousness, rose to the height of the ceiling. Spreading her arms and legs, she resembled a five-pointed star. Her quivering form vibrated the molecules about her in an outward spiral motion till she was surrounded by rings of phosphorous particles. Her voice of crystal covered the room like a dome.

"The night is filled with points of light.
   The ends of our fingers are set aflame.
   The moon in an indigo gown
   is wading in a sea of ink and silk.
   The boiling movements of our bodies
   swirl like an empress of silence.
   We three shadows of the moon."

The three shadows balanced themselves on the precipice of the morning. The haunting fog of their presence was illuminated. Once more they joined themselves at the table, clasping hands. A platter was brought forth and set before them, filled with a radiance of light, the sun. Their voices joined in unison to gather the harmonious litany.

"We three shadows of the moon,
   a woman's heart of triangle's dances,
   the fleeting somnambulant mood.
   The coffin beds of our hour
   is the swirling empress of silence.
   Our tongues touch in gold,

Our feathered romances lifted skyward
into the haunting gale of our voices.
We three shadows of the moon."

The shadows entered the fiery, luminescence of the sun. A whispered
sigh and a haunting hush, the candle extinguished and the room fell into
silence.

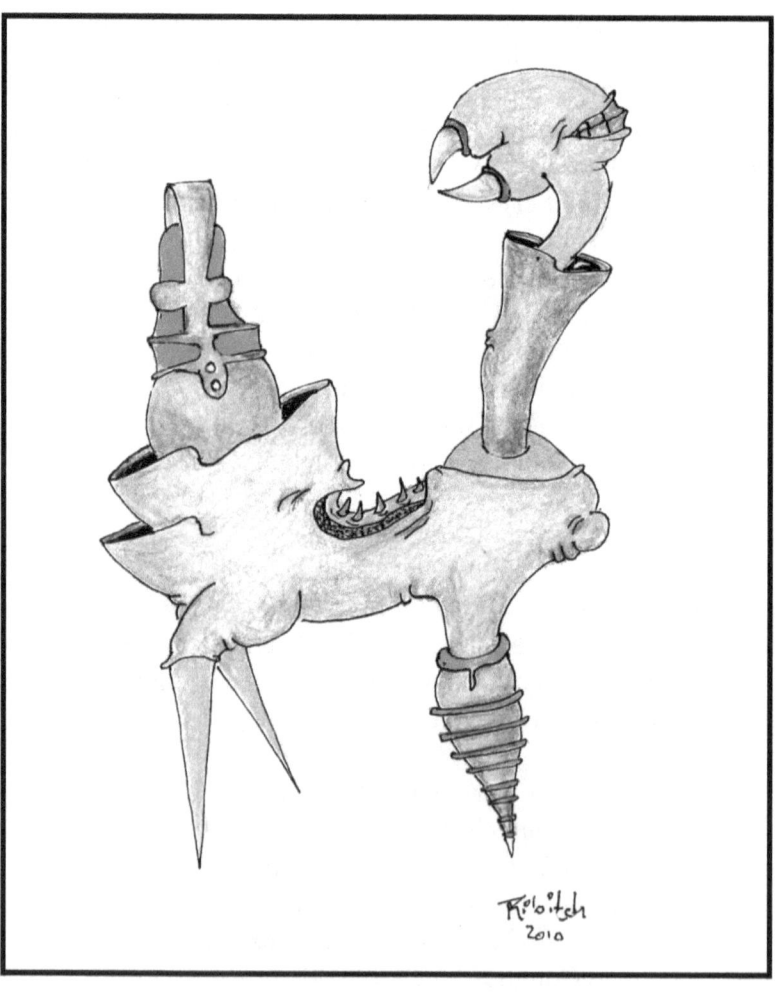

NEFFTANIA

It was after the first dawn,
with the coming of the delicate wind,
we saw her dance with the tide.
Her flaming hair and ghost arms were livid with seaweed
and the smell of fortune was exciting the membranes of her heart.
We stood distilled at the bottom of a gaping mouth.
The air of yesterday's storm lingered like a frightened newt,
wailing incantations, which quiver on the land.
We approached her smile
that hung around her waist like a dead bird.
We addressed her oblivion
and marked the souls of her feet with ribbons.
With these she danced, melted and mused,
with all the flaming hallways of possession,
gallant in each turn, she mounted a pale glass horse,
adorned with feathers and pearls.
We watched for hours, not daring to speak,
not daring to move for fear of upsetting the motion
of her breath. It was then she spoke to us…

"Each of you will in the season of blood,
display the glass of your voices
and squeeze the fire from the wind.
Each in your own moment, each in your own season.
I came to empty the faucets
That you keep hidden within your stare.
If anything is forgotten, it is also swollen.
Why do you weep so?
Do the swallows keep you from sleep?
You seething beast,
I have followed the corollas of death to the sea.
I have followed them in their dream of romance
And peppered the graves that weep with me."

The motion of the flat land exceeds the milestones of breath.

The sound of her breast swallowed the bones of silence.
A horse in the mist and a carnivore wind
is drawn on the fish's back.
Dancing with her shadow on a wilted spoon,
she froze within her throat the currency of the dawn.
The zones of madness with their coattails of thin light
are strange booty scattered across the pallor of simple sand.
Nothing could be divided or scalded
in the humming chatter of the bell.
The polar extremities, like a sigh
fell on her back and bled on the moon.
The sands of heaven heave forward,
coating a velvet floor with silence and dust.
She moves within the bag of her skin,
changing like a chameleon her shape.
She rides the shadow of a horse
and vomits milk in her open hand.
When asked her name, she replies...

"Nefftania!"

The silent Juggler passes Nefftania on her right,
holding balance in his teeth and shadows under his arms.
He coughs up blood on her thighs.
For this she smiles like smoke,
explaining the movement of fish
as they pass beneath the Jeweled horn.
The floor beneath her face is made of flesh and iron.
In this floor she reads the future as a medium
And casts them all with a waving of the hand and a clinch of the teeth.

"I saw your alabaster shoulder
as I passed beneath your hobbyhorse.
You glanced my way and your eyes burned a hole in my face.
I limped away, my eyes flaming.
I then collapsed to the earth,
but my shadow continued on a path made of snail.

My chin was linked by a chain to your ring finger."

The Old shaman who knew Nefftania by her shadow,
danced a ghost dance and whistled through his many lips.
Nefftania listened as if the wind felt beneath her skirt.

"Questions asked of the dawn refuse to see the shadow of birds
as they wander within the dead flames of silence.
This in the night in silver slippers, this is the drying moon."

Every time the dawn breaks
Nefftania glides into the wind of spacious conspiracy.
It is there she dines…
The silent juggler breaths in a poison air of skin,
Never ceasing to question the moon under Nefftania's breast.
So hollow is the sky with its clouds of dust.
So empty are the dreams that unfold with the dawn.
He weeps into his swollen hands
And all that he juggles becomes as moths approaching a flame.

"All of the death that clings to your feet
is filled with fog and the alabaster of clouds.
Fortune evades the moment of panic
Like the lips of my sex
Embracing the sand as if it were a wound,
As if the night would never end,
As if…
As if…
Follow me into the dream of Icarius!"

They followed Nefftania like a cloud,
each motion of her hips causing
the dislocation of the sky from the earth.
Each fling of her flaming arms disrupting
the caustic movement of the mind.
Swills of dilemma
and under the soft bellies of extreme excitation,

Each displayed the curves of dream
and the rudeness of the approaching dawn.
Ra Fantu, like a savage horn of a shadow,
whistles in the dark a melody.
It brings forth the warm worm images of Acanthus,
who owes so much to the moon.
The moon with its teardrop face swollen like a rose.
The moon is tied to the sky where lips end.
The travels of the dawn are caught on the edge of a horn.
The dormant dawn of claws,
The screaming dawn of elephant saxophone screams.
Ra Fantu gathers the veil of mists to carry it
to the dark side of the moon,
where waits Nefftania like an opal bowl of light.
Sunk deep within the earth,
the air sack of eyes lays in wait with swollen lips
for the night side of Nefftania's gown of fragile crows.
Her breasts protrude from the earth.
Her ancient smile attaches itself to the braid of fog,
to the decimated memory of her mouth.
The light of her composure extends with the waves
across the hollow landscape
and all that follows, drowns in the pleasure of her shadows.
The shadows of the veil trail across the sky and hang on tiny lips.
The lake is filled with frost, red as blood,
red as the sun that hangs beneath the arm of Nefftania.

"Nefftania, your napkin waist hugs the sky like a swallow's dream.
Where can I be on a night like this,
when all fortune lays strangled by the briars of your skirt?
Nefftania, Nefftania, call me when the owl's breath dies."

The glass boat of Nefftania's circular eyes
floats forth like a dirigible of white foam.
The evening of her throat is luminescent
and sits upon her tongue like the night,
like her skirt frozen in a sea of motion

and like the desert that bleeds beneath the surface.
Nefftania walked across her velvet purse of eyes.
Her polymorphic form fell into passion with the wind.
All those who would hunt out Nefftania are haunted by shadows.
Their eyes are stolen,
their quilted backs are penned with strange hieroglyphs.
Sometimes they are invisible to the naked eye
and at other times they are only visible
in the fading mist of the dawn.

Traveling beneath the moon in threes
they act out the trinity.
Their long combs trailing in the mist.
The tresses of their bones are collared
between the dusk and the dawn.
They who follow,
like shadows in the smoke of Nefftania's sex
swallow the dry ice of silence.
Nefftania looks over the horizon
for a place to lay her seed.
She wears her labia like a hat!

"Let me sing the sweet melodies of some distant time,
unchained from the fetters of calloused hands.
Songs of frogs and mermaids are murdered on the beach.
Let me strain my ears to hear the soft murmuring tide.
Let me walk in the blood of the morning
with my fingers tied to my waist like leeches.
Let me…"

The hourglass of Nefftania's waist exploded in the early hours
of a morning immersed in fever and reflection.
Her feet danced on and her songs fell from her lips like locusts.
She merged with the earth within the fronds of wakefulness,
her hands holding out in supplication to the sun,
a tiny crystal clock that could only speak of the past.
It was there in the loneliness of the desert sand, she wept.

"Now for me, in the season of must and smoke,
I seek my sleep like I seek the far flung shadows of my soul.
Now for me, in the season of ribbon and lace,
I seek the food of my thought in each grain of sand
that fills this desert that has poured from my belly
like jade worms who crawl to the horizon to die.
Now for me, in the season of lust and depravity
I Nefftania lay myself down to seek the slumber of snow."

MOISTIANBO

After an uneventful train ride, I was nearing my destination. Scientific study or pleasure, I was about to embark upon a most remarkable journey. I was to be met at the station by Dr. Louis DuVille, the esteemed professor of cultural anthropology, who would then guide me to my final destination, the island of Mostianbo. This island up till now was unknown to the outside world. It had been only recently discovered, hidden within a blanket of thick unmoving mist, off the coast of Northern California. This event had caused quite a stir in the media, for this body of land had eluded even the most sophisticated Satellite observations. Now I was to be amongst the first of a team of observers to record conditions on this remarkable island.

Dr. Louis DuVille was waiting on the platform and after vigorous handshakes and greetings he ushered me to a waiting car. "We must hurry!" he exclaimed to me. "The window of opportunity is indeed very short. Approach to the island can only be taken at certain hours and under very rare conditions. The tides are right this very night and we must make haste. I have a boat waiting for us, fully rigged with all the recording equipment that you may need. I will explain further in the car."

The excitement in Dr. DuVille's eyes as he spoke was very contagious. "The island, only discovered a few days ago, is full of anomalies, curious plant life, and its inhabitants are truly amazing," he explained. I could hardly contain my own excitement as he tried to describe what he had only heard by word of mouth. The only abatement to my delirious excitement would come with firsthand observation of this marvelous island called Mostianbo.

The island loomed before us, hidden by a shroud of mist so thick that it only appeared after we were almost upon its shores. A sonorous music could be heard, that seemed to float across the waves as if to greet us strangers in a strange land. It was soft and melodic, almost as if it were produced by electronic and synthetic instruments. I looked quizzically at Dr. DuVille, who in turn looked as equally baffled by this musical phenomenon. Our boat anchored just offshore and we took a skiff to the beach. At first glance there was nothing unusual about the beach-long stretches of sand, jutting rock and the interior cutoff from view by a wall of foliage and trees. But then something caught my eye, there was a slight shimmering hue about the sand, a slight glow that was almost undetectable to the eye. I reached down and picked up a handful of sand and let it sift through my fingers. The sand floated rather than fell, in a luminous cascade that resembled stars or bits of light. It took a full minute for the last luminescent grain to settle back upon the beach. I placed a small sample into a vial, for further analysis, and placed the vial into my backpack.

The music seemed to be coming from just beyond the trees, so we continued forward to discover its source. At the edge of the forest we stopped to examine the plant life that grew at the edge of the sand. The first plants we came upon were small, gelatinous succulents of about 6 inches in height that were festooned with small berry-like fruits. The young, unripe fruits were hard, yellow and about the size of a pea, while the ripe fruits were the size of my thumb and a bright blood-red in color. I picked one and held it to my nose; it had a sweet rosy smell with a hint of cinnamon. I bit into it and my mouth was instantly filled with a sensuous array of flavors, like none I have tasted before. I almost felt drunk with the richness of the flavor. The texture of the fruit was chewy like gum, but then it completely dissolved after about four minutes of chewing. The next plant was a flowering bush, whose blossoms were the shape of small birds hanging by their beaks. I examined these briefly, promising myself to make sketches of them later in my notebook. The music was louder now, and its source could now clearly be seen. The trees at the edge of the beach towered above us nearly 50 feet; the trunks of the trees were about ten inches in diameter and were covered with small holes of varying sizes. As the wind blew from offshore, it passed over the holes in the trees like air through a flute. The tones played off each other; the rising and falling of the wind gusts would change the level of the tones in the air. Quite remarkable music created from the natural environment.

As we moved further into the interior, our eyes were met by more wondrous sights. Just beyond the stand of musical trees we came across what appear to be the first signs of intelligent life. We came into a clearing of about 30 feet in diameter, clear-cut from the trees in a perfect circle. In the middle of the clearing there stood a totem. The totem circumference at the base was 3½ feet; its height must have been 75 feet or more. It was made of polished smooth black stone. It was very intricately carved with the shapes of some anterior lifeforms. These figures seemed to be laid out in the biogenesis of a species. They wound around each other in an erotic dance that seemed to be a continuous flow of sexual communication. The creatures seemed to be of a polymorphic nature as they blended and molded into the next. I walked the circumference of the totem, trying to follow the logic to how the figures were laid out. When I reached the point of view in which I had started, my senses felt a sudden shock. The figure of which I had begun my visual inspection had changed, or so it seemed. The change was subtle, as if it had moved. To confirm this phenomenon, I retrieved the digital camera from my pack and took a picture of the figure and the surrounding figures. I then marked a spot in the sand and walked slowly around the totem. Again the figure had changed. It was swallowed by, and was swallowing, the surrounding figures. I set up my tripod and took several pictures in a time-lapse mode to inspect this change. I called Dr. DuVille over to confirm my observations. The figures were indeed changing. They were metamorphosing one into the next in an exquisitely slow dance. I put my hand very lightly onto the surface of the totem. I expected the surface of the stone to be hard and cold, but instead it was warm, almost velvety in texture, and it moved! I could feel it pulse and shift. A living totem, pulsing out its own biogenesis, it was creating its own history in this moving stone flesh.

My heart was beating rapidly from the excitement of this incredible discovery. So lost was I in the meditation of the totem's movement that I began to feel a dislocation of my consciousness. It was as if I were being pulled into the biogenetic thread of this lifeform. I began to hear a voice that was not my own, but it was in my head as if it were my own thoughts. "We are phantoms," it spoke. "We are the empty spaces that fill themselves with the marvelous. We are the loose threads that began to unravel on the fabric of your reality." I opened my eyes and looked at my hand resting on the totem. The totem had wrapped several small tentacles around my fingers. "You are looking into the heart of me, of us, of yourself. You are surprised. You seem to have been expecting something else, something flesh and blood." The tentacle was now wound up to my elbow. "We are the stuff of your dreams, your wildest imaginings and your deepest desires."

"Why are you here?" I asked.

"Why are you?" questioned the totem.

"Because a new land was discovered, where none had been seen before," I replied. "Because the world had been thought to have been charted, and that there was nothing left to discover. I find myself caught in the dilemma of the curious."

The totem seemed to convey a sense comfort in our ability to find a bond of communication between us. "You speak as if discovery has become a rare commodity. Discovery is! It is the very fabric of my species. Today we are, tomorrow we will be…, and in between is the discovery of becoming." The end of the tentacle touched my face and explored my features. "Your face is rigid. The change that takes place is only subtle. The face of your birth is not too distant from the face you will wear at death. We are polymorphic. Yesterday my haunches rode high and I was a male; today I am female and my vaginal cavity secretes another species, which will in turn swallow me in its passing. I am a river of water that flows over ever-changing stones. I am and we are… just wisps of shadow that shift from one surface to another."

"How is it you exist?" I asked. "What is your sustenance? Do you eat food, drink water? What is it you dream?

"Sustenance is what you term as poetry; it is the law of entropy released from an envelope. You have taste buds, we have buds of taste. This totem is a complete biosphere in and of itself. Existence is what we dream, and dreaming is the breath of the biosphere."

"Are there any more of you on this island?" I asked.

"There are many such biospheres," the totem replied. "The dance of dreaming is not a solitary act. Our consciousness is separate, but our dreams are hyper-connected by a system of lobes far beneath the surface of the island. This is the way we communicate amongst ourselves. This is the way we sing the song of our genetic histories. If you sit with me for long enough I will tell you stories with as many endings as there are beginnings and endless possibilities of twists in plot. If you approach another such as myself, the tale will lead to a different conclusion altogether or may have a slight deviation in the structure of language. The linguistics may vary from one to another with fine threads that will weave a tapestry of the possibility of a multilevel sense of reality. Reality changes as often as the surface of our skin and the polymorphic structure of our form. The time of migration nears, we will be in movement soon."

The tentacle receded and again became part of the flow. Dr. DuVille touched my shoulder and I felt no more connection with the totem. "What is it?" he asked. "You too seemed caught up in a trance."

"It spoke to me," I said as I turned to him. "You did not hear it? It's alive! This is truly amazing; we have met with the indigenous life of this island. There is so much to learn here. I'm trembling, look at my hand." Indeed my hands were shaking. The song of the trees began to rise in pitch and tempo. The winds from offshore had picked up and were creating a crescendo of sound that was becoming unbearable.

"We must get back to the boat!" shouted Dr. DuVille. "I don't think I can bear much more of this sound. My ears are beginning to hurt." We picked up our things and proceeded back toward the beach. Before leaving the clearing, I turned back toward the totem. It began to quiver all over, and then it began to twist and contort. Pulling itself from the ground, it then simply floated away, dividing and separating as it disappeared into the interior.

THE VAMPYRE

The ladle of the moon sopping up blood,
where discreet silence lies in webbed hands.
The marks in the earth are footpads
that race across monstrous screams,
the howls in the bones of quiet.

The ladle of the moon,
the ruby red lips are parted
in the excited erotic passion marking the mirror
with the frost of breath tracing out the lines
of a haunting moon rising from a sleep
that is caught in the throat,
that is caught in the serrated
poison of lost dreams.

The marks on the throat,
they mark the time, an eternity of secret scrolls.
The ladle of the moon napping in a bed of cold satin,
drowsy and drunk with fever,
the mist seeping from eyelids
beneath the door that has sprung.

The ladle of the moon, dipping into death,
awakening to the howl of silence.
The trees stand bare, testaments to a lonely somnambulist,
whose lips have parted from white flesh,
pale as a ghost moon,
pale as the cold ash of snow.

Lamia Sanctus, Burning a cross,
singing under the moonlit stars.
Ashes that float to the earth
leave the footprints of wolves.
The ladle of the moon, the wooden spike
turned upward to spear heaven,

who will drip a trail of blood,
that will wander to barren hillsides.

Lamia Sanctus, the unholy rising of corpora.
their fortunes are read in empty teacups.
The ladle of the moon, dipping into the split-open chest,
where the heart beats on wooden doors
opened up to the sweet whisper of dark dreams.

Lamia Sanctus, the ladle of the moon,
a scar upon the sky opened up like a sarcophagus
of aged old men and bats,
of aged old women and wolves.
Their wrinkles are caught in time,
caught within the shallows of shadow.
The ladle moon, echoes in an empty hallway,
like footsteps dropping to dusty pews.

Lamia Sanctus, the crooked cross burning under the moon.
The wolfen scream, arms spread out in ceremonial rictus.
Lamia moon, ladle of dreams,
dipping into the dripping paradise, a gypsy hollow.
The wagons filled with fear, a wet fear, red and warm.
The waxy pallor peeling back under the corollas of wolfbane.
Ladle moon, Lamia Sanctus.

The priests cower under their pews,
holding forth their collars.
Poor Van Helsing…
Poor Harker…
Poor Rinfield…

Fear of the moon settled between their shoulder blades,
angling their mirrors inward.
Lamia moon, wearing a cloak of black,
lowering the shade of darkness with long bony fingers,
white like the face of the moon.

The paradox of Nosferatu, howling in the bones of quiet.

Ladle moon, Lamia Sanctus…
Listen!
The soft inviting whisper, locked in the grip of embrace.
Cold as icy death, white as the moon,
or bones, or tombs.
The trembling gypsy moon, veiled in the Romanian fog.

Ladle moon, Lamia Sanctus…
Listen!
The soft inviting whisper.

TRAVEL ABROAD

1

The Journey Begins

5:30 in the morning, and the air was filled with cobwebs. My breath was heavy. It fell from my lungs like lead weights. For some torturous reason I must do as I was bid. Even if I could change the direction of the wings of chance, I could not have turned an inch from my destiny or the gloved hand of some nameless thing. I have feared this moment for many weeks. I have feared the approach of something veiled in the smoke of secrecy. The fear ate at my face and tore at my lips.

It was upon my entrance to the Hotel Ruby that this deep foreboding shadow fell upon my shoulder, and my sanity fell to the wind. From the grey mists of reality to the edge of an inexpiable illusion, the haunted forms of some babbling delusion lay sway to the foolish wanderings of my feet. I can't say what brought me through those doors. A nervous unswayable desire overtook me. I could feel the glass eye of oblivion hiding in the reeds of caution. Laying in the naked sway above my gaze, the sign of this cold tomb listed in the wind and sighed for the years hidden in its shadow.

The lobby of the Hotel Ruby was filled with a thick fog. Bellboys moved robotically back and forth, serving no one. It was my shock to discover, when attempting to ask one of these mute bellboys, that they were plaster mannequins. I whirled about and fell back against the wall when one of the plaster mannequins turned solemnly and pointed to a staircase. I moved up the stairs that could have been a giant tongue. Into the heavy darkness and into the solemn silence of shadow's room, room thirty six. The door quivered and wept to itself. I felt my hand take hold of the knob as if it were a gun. Inside, the smell of ermine and the fossilized remains of destiny filled the air. My eyes opened to an opal blackness that confounded my throat and froze my lingering form.

Hovering about mid-sight was an old man sitting on a small polished brass cube. He was naked, except for an earring that was a dead bird. His eyes were set deep within his face; deep within the radiant glass void beyond; deep within the vomiting luminescent shadows. His mouth hung in silence. His shadow hung on a coat hanger in the corner of the room. I walked around him; his translucence undulated with the hues of the cube. He glanced at me with tattooed eyes. The breath that fell from his nostrils exploded in the wind. I approached him with cautious indifference. His lips curled up in a mocking turbulent smile. They parted, revealing stone teeth and bitter laughter.

"Why have I been brought here?" I questioned. "What reason is this vision brought to mind?"

The smile faded from his face. His lips pushed together forcing the bones in his face to rise. "From now on," he replied, "the fields of chance will conqueror the alleys of the mind. You will venture forth into a questionable reality. The vulture's laughter will be at your shoulder." He reached into the air and retrieved a velvet box, and this he handed to me. I turned it over in my hand. It seemed to bark out some danger or mystery that alluded to something cold like frost. I opened it, and there inside I found a ticket bound for Papua New Guinea aboard the schooner *"L'Esprit."*

I found myself sitting in the musty hold of the *L'Esprit*, my heart was in suspended animation, my eyes not seeing the unfolded mirrors that lay at my feet. The shore slipped away into its own oblivion as discreetly as if it were a moth folding its wings. The soft silence became the turn of things found there in the searing shadows. They invaded the gossamer silences that seemed to cling to the air. For every motion there was a texture. For every hallway there was a thousand exits, each with a different masked figure, and not wanting to enter one or the other, I wandered endlessly on.

2

3rd Day Out
40 Leagues Above the Tropic of Cancer

Daylight was coughing itself up from the sea. Like a thousand women's hips, it emerged from the darkness. I could not sleep, or else I could not get myself awake. I stood on the bow of *L'Esprit*, my eyes grasping at the legs of a new day. It was in my reverie that a crushing sob came to my ears. I peered deep into the mist, and my breath followed my gaze. The mist obscured everything except for the rising sobs coming from somewhere out at sea. The sobs rose and fell in ever increasing crescendos, and I searched out into the distance for some sign of their presence. My eyes could not penetrate the thick morning mist.

At first it appeared as a thin silhouette, outlined on the field of gray. Slowly it gave in to a form so transparent; it almost escaped my attention. It was a woman, veiled in the mist. She appeared to me as a faint escaping shadow, transparent and death-like. Floating in the reaches of the waves, she was pristine and luminescent. As her form became more distinct, so too did the clarity of her sobs. I leaned out over the rail towards her, edging to grasp at the hidden mirrors of her cries. I wanted to touch her, to feel the spiderwebs of her hair, but she hovered just beyond my reach. I could extend myself no further for fear of falling into the sea. Her insistent sobs swallowed the air and crushed the mist. The tide of her cries enveloped all of the motion in the sea and held it still in silence. Her bodily form was shrouded in fine silk. Her eyes were like glass flames. Her lips parted and quivered with each sob and tears lay like dead fish on her cheeks. Her body edged up against the *L'Esprit*, noisily abusing the hull. I reached for her, but she avoided my touch. My heart felt as if it were breaking in two. She appeared so wretched and lost. Her sadness fell over me like a blanket of lead. I wanted to flee, but I wanted to know why she wept so violently. I asked her why she was weeping, and she replied, "I am a shadow of the mist, and light eludes me; it swallows my heart, and because all of the faces hidden in ancient doorways are so decayed and fossilized, they no longer remember their births. My destiny, like theirs, appeals to the laughing winds."

Her heart was cast into splinters, and she followed each sliver with eager anticipation. The blood-red of her lips swam in the slow sensation of her ambivalence. She waltzed on the waves like a dancer who could no longer find her feet. "Can there be an end to your long solitude?" I asked.

"Only when the sands rise out of this sea," she replied. "For all my years seeped in this misfortune, I would seek my rest. An eternity of my immortality is stretched across my eyes like an amniotic sac. It is there the foam of the sea ends, and death is squandered like so much loose change."

I turned from her and stared at the descending moon. "When will it end?" I asked. "Or is this to be what fortune there is, and am I to be hurled without any resemblance into an uncertain destiny not of my choosing?"

"You've seen my form," she replied, "and that is all that can be said. Even that is more than what is granted to all the sailors who have sailed past me. Their coming and going is as the wind or a ghost of some impossible illusion. They pass and stare out into the night, hoping for one glimpse of my shadow. Maybe one or two will catch sight of my form skirting along the edges of silence, but nevermind, even they lose their minds." The cold was cutting into me like a razor; I moved back as if I were shocked by my own reflection that was shattered and weeping. My mind felt like it was losing its grip. I started to call out to her, but she was gone.

3

Auckland New Zealand

L'Esprit limped into Auckland, New Zealand, just after dark. The captain thought it was best under the circumstances. Seventeen persons were dead on the boat. On the voyage, they were overcome by an acute hysteria. Not even the ship's doctor could tell what caused it. It was as if the sea had come to claim them. It took their minds and left the shells of their bodies laughing at their shadows. I saw one occurrence and sorely wished that my eyes had not witnessed it. A child of the age of ten, as she played upon the deck, was suddenly seized by a quick and violent tremor. Her eyes rolled back in her head, and she faced the sea. She threw back her head and began to laugh. The laughter fell from her mouth in pools, and then she collapsed, paralyzed with a sardonic grin. Three days later, she died with that twisted smile on her face. Each one that died displayed the same manner of hysterical laughter followed by *paralytic sardonicus* and then death. The captain tried numerous times to bury the bodies at sea, but every morning they were again lying on their deathbeds. We docked in Auckland to get rid of the dead bodies. The captain said he will pay some locals to carry the bodies into the interior and entomb them in the bottomless pits that are rumored to exist there. The rest of us were bound to the ship till it departed.

4

The Palace Bar
Sidney Australia

The captain invited me to have a drink with him at one of the local establishments known for its colorful clientele and its famous Fugu-laced martinis. He assured me the place was safe, but once my eyes adjusted to the darkness, the blood stains on the floor said something else. Six apes lounged in the corner; they smoked cigars and played a card game with blank cards. The air was filled with hisses and cries. The apes snickered and winked at one another as we entered. The room smelled of something dead. Three nuns were nailed to the wall above the bar. Their habits were raised and sardines were taped to their sex. From their Cornets hung deflated balloons. Their faces were painted like whores, pasty white masks, with rouge and deep red lipstick. The eye makeup was smeared down their cheeks, giving witness to their recent tears. The bartender wore a crown of thorns and a latex body suit that resembled lizard skin. We took a seat and the captain nodded to the bartender with a knowing glance of familiarity. The bartender then turned and prepared our drinks and delivered them to our table. He set the glasses down, bending close to the captain's ear whispering something and looking me directly in the eye. I shuddered; the nuns moaned. The martinis were garnished with the puffer fish eyes that sat on a soft pillow of fugu.

I drank the dank liquid, sucking down the puffer's eye and the fugu pillow. The apes in the corner chuckled, glancing in my direction. One of them winked at me and grinned, his fangs yellow-brown. The nuns sighed; The bartender coughed;The captain snickered; I blacked out.

5

New Caledonia

I found myself far off into the jungle; the light of the sun was obliterated by the canopy overhead. One would think that light was

143

but a haze on the shoulder of a sumptuous sensation. Sounds exploded on the edge of silence. The breath of violence clung to that blanket of green. It interloped every inch of earth. The bleeding moon that rises from the Horn failed to conclude the day. I heard cries of the unseen. They mocked my movements, just beyond the emerald wall. Violence was unseen like a forest fire. I had not planned to disembark here in New Caledonia. What was this excursion into the dark green shadow, but a wound on the eye of destiny?

It was two days ago, just south of New Caledonia, and the night was falling off my shoulders like dust. I was weeping. I was wearing my body for the first time, and it was full of holes. I sat alone except for the ghosts that hung themselves over the side. Their screams clung to the railing; Their faces hung in the air. Their endings exist for an eternity on the tides of this loneliness. I wept in my hands, seeing nothing but the blindness of my thoughts.

I heard a faint tapping sound coming my way. A very tall man accompanied the noise. He was dressed in a white panama suit. A cane held in his right hand was the source of the noise. The cane was of an elaborate design, with a dragon frozen in a pose of erotic repulsion. It was gold and ivory, and the eyes were the eyes of the man who possessed it. The eyes were the eyes of flame, desire and the utmost extremities of violence. He bore a mustache that curled around his long pointed nose like a snake. The structure of his face was like chiseled stone, - cold and stoic, - as white as death. His mouth curved up in a brooding malevolent smile. The flash of his eyes burned into the face of the earth and turned to ash the blood of silence. He stopped in front of me, as still as stone, his menacing eyes coldly upon me. He dropped a calling card at my feet. As suddenly as he appeared, he was gone. Only a wisp of his cologne remained. I picked up the calling card to read:

Variétés de Rêves Merveilleux
Le Vampir du les Morts
Louis DuVille

I turned the card over in my hands; it felt more like a dead bird than the paper card that it was. On the back of the card was a handwritten note that read, "When the ship docks, disembark; at the south end of the village you will find a clearly marked path. Follow this to the end. The ship will be held for you."

So it was in this frame of mind that I left the ship and ventured into the green fear and the unknown death that I felt surely awaited me. It was this same sane mind that I question without relief. It was so silent here, not at all what I expected. There was no chattering of birds, or the screaming of monkeys, nor was there the buzz of insects, but only my hysterical breath within the wall of this extreme silence. My heart felt swallowed by a night of flame that was the sweet extremes of violence and the touch of its elastic barriers. I listened to my heartbeat floating on the wind. I listened, with the wind at my back, haunting the very edges of my ears. I walked in the very shadows that lurk in the moment. I stood on the inky precipice of some unknowable presence. Breath upon breath I walked, and there in the shallows of a gasp that filled the space between the turbulent jungle and me, a shadow lingered.

The pathway had all but disappeared in the undergrowth; I felt the giddy sensation of fear as I contemplated being lost in this disturbing maze of emerald jungle. After a time I came to a clearing. An old woman sat in a large wicker chair. She possessed a wide grin, or else it possessed her. In her hand she held an ancient glass, round and foggy. Within the glass was held my glance. Within my glance were the frozen tomorrows of a poison. The old woman rolled her head back and gave out a laugh, a jackal's laugh. Her eyes rolled to the side; her tongue groped at the air in an insane gesture.

"A quiet summer," she laughed. "It is a quaint quietude on the ends of my lips."

"Why have I been summoned here?" I asked, shivering with fear.

"For your destiny," she replied. "and a whiff of the wind, and a phantom of your shadow in a dark corner." She held up the glass so that the filtered light danced in the reflection. "You come for a voice that never ends. You come and go like the vapors that fall from your nostrils." She held the glass to me and leaned back in her chair, laughing to the emptiness of the jungle. Her smile creased her face. "You will have an opportunity for its use. It will lead toward uncertainty and answer the questions that haunt your sleepless nights." She closed her hand on the glass globe, and when she opened it, all that remained was ash. She took an envelope from beneath her skirt and placed the ashes inside of it. She sealed the envelope and handed it to me. She smiled in a malevolent grandmotherly way and said sternly, "That is all!"

6

East China Sea

It was nearly midnight; the deck of *L'Esprit* was covered with snakes. I watched the East China moon raise itself up to chase the stars. With each moment that same moon within the same sky eluded the mystery of the East China heat that consumed my body and soul.

The East China Sea, gateway to the serpent's mouth. The dragons of delusion and the haunting mystery that counts the fortunes of the night on the surface of this mirrored sea. The East China Sea is a violent tremor that stalks the tiger with a double bladed sword. It seeks to wrench from the sky, its moon, its desire and the dreams of fortune on the serpent's tongue. The East China Sea!

7

Shanghai, China

To cough with opium lungs, a fire of flowers sent to death on the legs of a turtle. The dark passages of willow bark and the breath of silent things suffer of a broken wing in the twilight hour woven with great speed. I sat in my room, looking from a window, smelling the footsteps of Death. I seen an old man carrying a wooden leg. From his beard hung burning ropes. He muttered and stumbled in the dark. I seen four children hauling the mutilated corpse of a donkey. They sang a song that shattered all other sounds.

> "Dance, dance we dance
> Around grandfather's grave,
> Digging, digging, digging,
> We dig in the shadow of a horse,
> Whose false head remembers.

> All the quaint little pictures
> Laughing, laughing all laughing…"

My room was filled with shadows and sobs. The only company I have had since my arrival are the three men chained to the wall, and their death before my coming was no consolation. The bells tolled everyday at three in remorse and anguish. The frustrated screams in the hollow night filled my room with voices. They spoke in harmonious unison of follies and deeds of valor and…

> Dance, dance we dance
> Around grandfather's grave
> Chasing his teeth with hickory sticks
> Waltzing under the moon
> With the shadows of a dream
> Laughing, laughing, all laughing…"

8

Nanchang China

The Emperor of Nanchang hinted at the mystery of the highly decorated box. With a wink he grabbed at my attention. The smile on his face lingered forever. He motioned me over to view the box with a fat stubby finger. "The dragon does not live forever," he exclaimed. "Neither do the mazes that puzzle a questionable mind. Here, my friend, is a gift of kings, a whisper on a cold night or a secret that unfolds." He turned his head, motioned to a slave, then turned back to me. "Do you wager on the snakes?" he asked. "Humor me, if you will, a game or two."

I glanced at his eyes, which flashed a dangerous look. "A game?" I asked. His grin seemed to roam around the room, but his eyes lay on only me. I felt terrified. He reached into his toga and pulled out two snakes, a red one and a blue one. He held them out to me.

"Choose a snake," he said. "The blue ones are nice…"

I took the blue snake from his hand, and it immediately wound up my arm. I looked on in shock as it wound higher and higher, inching its way toward my face. I shivered, and the blue snake curved itself around my neck, its head now only inches from my ear. I wanted to brush it away, but I could not move a muscle. The blue snake entered my ear, and my brain felt as if it would explode. Swirls of light clouded my vision, and a symphony of sound shook my bones. I spun dizzily and fell to the floor. When I awoke, the Emperor was placing the snakes back into his toga. "Luck is with you for the moment, my friend," He said with an air of dry humor. He rolled a ball across the table. The emperor smiled as though his teeth were made of lead. "My dear friend, you hesitate to pick up your winnings. Perhaps you could put them within that envelope you carry in your pocket, with the ashes." His smile cut me off midstream. The serpents within his toga smiled out at me with the same heavy smile as his. "Oh please, you offend," his voice cackling off into the darkness.

There was a period of silence that invaded a space in time and it hovered in the air like raw fish. He then broke the silence with a voice that was barely an audible shudder in the darkness. "Your journey will be fraught with dangers and strange uncontrollable dilemmas that will resemble a dream more than reality, but dream and reality are separated by a mere thread of distance, and if the thread is broken and the two collide then… well let me just say that all that is revealed will be a cloud of smoke. Remember this: a moon that is full may not be what you think." Then he was gone.

9

Kun Lun Mountains, Tibet

My eyes filled with water that froze in tiny rivulets upon my cheeks. I glanced about me with nervous intent. The hum of the wind filled my ears and drove my mind toward the edges of oblivion, the same oblivion that sits upon the shoulders of the wind, and the same oblivion that is a haunting stone at the bottom of the sea. My ears were filled with the recurring sweet whisper: "you hesitate to pick up your winnings…" My mind was filled with the memory of the Emperor's face, his stone smile and his haunting glance remained embossed in my mind. Not even the jutting ragged edges of the Kun Lun could shake it loose.

My first hours in the Kun Lun appeared before me as my first hours of birth. The shocking light that hangs from the sky, clings to the

148

whiteness of the pale-death snow. The shadows of the silence were like guillotines mimicking the angular lines that have crossed my face with the coming of age. The Kun Lun, with its demanding cold presence, enveloped me like a shroud. Each stone was placed like a chess piece on a demented game board. I stood near the black queen, who stood near the black bishop. Monolithic they stood, rising out of the snow, challenging the torrent of rain and the sweet illusions of my destiny. My presence here amongst the shadows, where the faces of stone linger in the quiet passion of the full moon, left no shadow cast on the ground. The opal drapery of the moon fell across the ground with an elongated laughter.

My eyes bit at the darkness. A howl bit at the silence of the mountain pass. I felt my nerves ride my back like electric shocks. This was the edge of the world, that like the edge of a smoked glass window, marked the edge of a wound that was a path marked by the snowy blood of the Kun Lun. This seemed to be my hour and it was folded up in a white silk, a white silk with the initials L.D.V. embroidered in the corner in blood red. My hand felt inside my pocket, and a small white card fell beneath my fingers like the wing of a bird. I traced the raised letters with my fingers: *Louis DuVille!* A blanket of white snow draped like a thin veneer of skin across my shoulders. My mental state was agitated. The nerve endings screamed to the outer layers of my skin.

I huddled myself beneath a stone monolith. My senses searched the air for something that seemed hidden and precariously balanced upon the edge of reality. The Kun Lun ignored my presence and drifted off onto a holograph of a dream. Something moved in the shadows. A form neither solid nor transparent lifted itself from the snow and reached to touch my face. My mouth opened to scream, but what sound there was lay frozen in the whiteness of the Kun Lun.

I fell into a slumber.

10

Kashgar, Sinkiang

I awoke from a fitful slumber. My head felt the raging scream of being divided in two. The left side of my face awoke in a small grey room. It lay on a table tacked down with small black nails. A group of guards sat in a semicircle with unsmiling faces. On the opposite side of the room sat a man whose head was covered with a black cloth. A voice filled with gravel shook me from my reverie of insistent juxtaposition. "So we meet again…" The voice came from the hidden face under the black cloth. "This time you seem to be at a disadvantage." He tapped an elaborate cane against the floor. The head of the cane was a dragon in a pose of erotic revulsion.

"Louis," I whispered.

"You have come at a most opportune time," he hissed, his voice almost reptilian beneath the black cloth. "It is the time of the Year when the Kobdo monks march forth from the Altai Mountains of Mongolia chanting their insidious litanies. In this region they are known as the Brotherhood of the Scorpions. They travel by foot over a thousand miles of treacherous terrain, led by blood-red scorpions tied to silver cords. They have no eyesight, with their eyes having been removed at birth in preparation of their destiny. All of Kashgar flee from the city as they have done for over ten thousand years, and I await their return as I've done for an equal amount of time. I leave you now to wait. You will hear them coming, by their song and by the scurrying of tiny scorpion feet."

11

The Garden

The right side of my face laid in a garden blanketed by the smell of poppies. The afternoon sun soothed my cheek with warmth. Above me, from a tree hung a coat of frail clouds, and a sweet music fell from the sleeves and drifted with a circular motion into my ear. I opened my half-mouth and butterflies issued forth, large black butterflies with gold-tipped wings and ivory horns protruding from their skulls. A voice drifted to my ear from the coat of clouds hung from the tree: "You really must make ready now. They will come for you soon."

"Who will be coming for me?" I asked

"The children of course," replied the voice. "Your body has already been shipped to a small boat that waits on the Caspian Sea. The left side of your face I'm afraid has fallen into the hands of a very dangerous situation." I started to ask for an explanation but already the singing voices could be heard approaching…

> "Dance, dance, we dance
> Around grandfather's grave
> His bones light up like the moon
> His face a silent slumber
> We hit the air with hickory sticks
> Laughing, laughing, all laughing."

My one eye glanced about. The familiarity of those small voices startled me. The rising and falling crescendos of their song burned my ears.

> "Dance, dance, we dance
> Around grandfather's grave
> Whittling the branches' arms
> Setting fire to faces
> Rolling from sea to sea
> Laughing, laughing, all laughing."

The children were ghostly pale under the light. They carried upon their shoulders dead pianos, executed by having their wires removed. In silence they wept for their silenced keys.

12

Kashgar, Sinkiang

I faced the grey wall in waiting stillness. My left ear in listening repose. I could hear far off in the distance a faint scratching sound. Behind the scratching, in a growing wail, the Kobdo monks shuffled in an almost silent whisper. Their feet were wrapped in colored silks. My ear could ascertain the tap, tap of an insidious carved cane moving toward the oncoming scurrying sound of the arachnoid's oblivion. I called out in the emptiness, "Louis, Louis, tell me why? Louis?" Just a dim laughter was my only answer.

13

The Garden

"Dance, dance, we dance
Around grandfather's grave
Like a somnambulist drifting in the fog
Like the set sound of frogs
We hover in dark slumber
Laughing, laughing, all laughing."

The persistence of memory lingered like a weathered coat, where moths house themselves in hibernation. It hung above me like a waiting guillotine. The voice from the coat interrupted my reverie. "You seem to be perplexed, as if some vague dream has invaded your mind.

The right side of my face screwed up with an expression of doubt. "Who's that singing?" I asked

"Perhaps your salvation," the weathered coat replied.

14

The Caspian Sea

I could feel my body lying gently upon a warm surface and the gentle rocking of a boat. Headless as I was, I felt acutely aware of the presence of others within the room. My hand reached out searching until it at last grasped a sleeve. I held onto the hand with a deep desperation, as it was my only link with the concrete. At last the hand opened my own and traced with a fingertip the recognizable letters of words. "I am Captain Surry," it traced. "Your body is aboard the fishing trawler *Shallow Breath*. You have been in our company for three weeks. Your unfortunate condition is a temporary one, I hope."

I fumbled with his hand, tracing my question in his. "Where is my head; what has been done with it?"

"I'm afraid I don't have that answer," he nervously traced into my palm. "I have been instructed that the utmost care is to be administered in resolving the separation. Please feel free to express your needs." I felt him leave the room, and an overpowering solitude took me over.

15

Kashgar, Sinkiang

The first of the Kobdo monks entered the room along with Louis. They quickly moved to my blind side and began speaking in hushed tones. I could only make out bits and pieces of their conversation, like "...do you think he will survive?" "...staple it to the mounting board...," "...wrapped in silk to be burned..." and "...find the rest, find the rest, it must be complete."

I strained my eye to see my company. Louis turned and smiled at me. "Ah, my friend, the time has arrived." He spoke with a slight hint of irony in his voice. "We shall prepare you soon, but first let me introduce you to master Ki." An imposing monk stepped forth, bowing low. His lips parted in a wide grin. Upon each tooth was pasted a photograph so that his smile resembled a gallery of strangers. He let his smile linger too long. The Photographs began to speak to me.

First Photograph: "The ancient history of misery sits upon a leaf ,smoking the incense of time."

Second Photograph: "The amount of waves that will exchange clothes with the scorpions."

Third Photograph: "The envelope, please."

First Photograph: "A game of snakes?"

Fourth Photograph: "You will tell us..."

Fifth photograph: "...where the journey ends?"

Sixth photograph: There is a wall of blood in Madrid."

First Photograph: "A game of snakes?"

Second photograph: "It is our pleasure."

First photograph: "A game of snakes?"

Seventh photograph: "I am the seventh photograph of the seventh photograph."

First Photograph: "A game of snakes?"

16

The Garden

The children gathered, giggling. They held cages filled with birds of different varieties. They all joined hands and began to dance in a circle around my face,

> "Dance, dance, we dance
> Around grandfather's grave
> Like stones gathered in a meadow
> We stare at our shadows
> Crossing the abyss of leaves,
> Laughing, laughing, all laughing."

17

Tabriz, Iran

There was some kind of commotion that I was not totally aware of. My body had been upon the Caspian Sea. I had been blindly pacing the deck when my body was suddenly grabbed and taken below. The captain signed into my palm that I was to be taken away, perhaps to join with my other parts. My body was wrapped in soft silks and hurriedly taken across the country. It was explained to me later that I was in Tabriz, Iran, beneath a fabric shop.

I was aware of some great anxiety. It was nothing that was said or done, but rather a feeling that clung to the air like a remorseful bandage. I could feel that my body was stored away with bolts of cloth. The texture of fine knits lay against my side and the sensuous itch of wool was laid across my chest. I felt helpless and alone, trapped as I was, headless and without control. I wanted to scream, but without a mouth, the scream just puddled in my chest like a stagnant pool of water. I wanted to cry, but without eyes, my tears only added to the pool, creating a sea of despair that flooded my body.

18

New Delhi, India

My right eye twitched. I felt quite excited; the dancing children, who always seemed to be in a state of laughter, had taken me in their arms and transported me south. New Delhi was alive with activity as we passed through the marketplace. The stench of dung hung in the air. The buzz of voices rose like a sonorous hum. The shadows of faces lengthened and shortened like a woven matt.

As we made our way through the streets, the children clacked their sticks together and with every gesture of their arms, faces turned. The weathered stares quickly retreated from my glance as if they knew that my voyage was marked by their own dreams. So we moved through the streets, the clatter of their feet upon the cobbles made the song of the dance:

> "Dance, dance, we dance
> Around grandfather's grave
> Singing the songs of spiders
> Reciting the ballads of the dead
> Clicking our sticks like our bones
> Laughing, laughing, all laughing."

The children took great care to turn my one good eye to see all they encountered. The exotic smells of curry and butter filled the air. Milk flowed from fountains where old women gathered up the white liquid in bowls made of clay. Men bowed their heads and made signs in the air to protect themselves. Only the children took joy in the event of my passage through the streets. They joined in the parade clapping their hands:

> "Dance, dance, we dance
> Around grandfather's grave
> Penny whistles play in the night air
> Offerings of milk and honey
> Tables are set for the feast
> Laughing, laughing, all laughing."

19

Kuldja, Sinkiang

We rode in a carriage north to Kuldja, Louis and Ki sat silently across from me. They swayed back and forth like little dolls. The shadows were lengthening across their faces, giving them the appearance of falseness, of masks that never lost their grins. The left portion of my face laid in a box of glass, and around it were seven black scorpions, each wearing a jeweled band. It occurred to me that the monks of Kobdo were shape-shifters, taking on the form of scorpions. It also became clear that they desired the envelope that was, I presumed, still with my body.

Louis leaned forward, tapping on the glass. "Well, my friend, I do hope you can see the situation clearly. We wish to have the envelope that came into your possession in New Caledonia. You have presented us with a problem, but one that is not insurmountable." He smiled, throwing back his lips. The curvature of his tongue rolled back over his upper lip then flicked downward like a snake over the bottom.

20

Tahcheng, China

The road to Tahcheng was like a haunting memory: it rose and fell with the passing strangers on the road. Each one was a hushed dream behind a veil of smoke. We passed an old man, who seemed to totter and almost fall. At the exact moment when his balance became unhinged, a small dog would run forward and nudge him into place. Then the scene would begin again. "This has been going on for more than a century," Louis sighed. He leaned over the box and smiled. "It is said that if ever he fell, his body would pass through the earth and at that moment…ah how I should put it, the mirror would break." He touched the obscene cane to the side of his nose and winked. He leaned from the carriage, calling out to one of the guards: "Kill the dog!"

21

Tabriz, Iran

Sometimes I find my arms caught within a dream. Sometimes I find my shadow sewn to the inner circles of my dilemma. Sometimes I find my unheard voice down dark haunted halls. Sometimes I can feel the hollows of my eyes searching the varying contrasts of a dream for the seething flow of ancient oceans. But now? Now all of my sometimes are held in suspended animation, frozen like an old and crumbling photograph. But sometimes... sometimes the wind hits the walls, and they begin to fall.

22

Tahcheng, China

Louis leaned over me with his haunting smile. The monk whose teeth were photographs grinned crowds of strangers. I wanted to cry for the old man, who no longer had anyone to hold him erect. He staggered back and forth, grabbing at whatever handhold would keep him aloft. His screams shattered the air as he plummeted from place to place like a manic pinball. "It's unlikely he'll fall," Louis commented with a shrug. "His desire to maintain a delicate balance is an old affair. We've just changed the pattern of the dance." Louis tapped his cane and the journey resumed.

23

Bombay, India

The right side of my face was laid out on a silk pillow; laughter filled the air like a thick fog.

"Dance, dance, we dance
Around grandfather's grave

Lifting waves of laughter
Floating on a sea of dream
Laughing, laughing, all laughing."

Bombay, like New Delhi, was crowded with outstretched hands and eyes full of hunger.

"Dance, dance, we dance
Around Grandfather's grave
Lifting dust like a blanket
Offering our clocks to the wind
Laughing, laughing, all laughing."

The children's eyes were aglow with a vibrant joy. With each clack of the sticks, the crowd became more jubilant. At each refrain of their song the crowd swayed and raised their hands.

"Dance, dance we dance
Around grandfather's grave
Testing the ball lightning
Swinging from the stars
Laughing, laughing, all laughing."

As we passed the outskirts of Bombay, thousands of whispering voices could be heard singing…,

"Dance, dance we dance
Around grandfather's grave…"

24

Antaly, Turkey

The overland journey to Turkey had been a hard and taxing ordeal. My body had been made as comfortable as could be expected, but the roads were bad, and storms plagued the way like hellhounds. The sights of a foreign land, even in dreadful weather, might have soothed me, but in blindness I had to travel. Without my senses to guide me, I felt lost on an endless horizon. Was it day or night? The rains were cold and wet no matter what time of day. To smell nothing, to see nothing had left me in such an agitated state. I was plagued with questions that no one could answer. Why was I aware of anything? Why was my mind attached to my body like a leech? Questions evaded my curiosity like the fox evades the hounds. But it is well known what would happen to the fox if he was caught in the jaws of the hounds, and the answers to my questions should be left unanswered.

It was signed into my hand that, when the morning came, my body would be taken across the Black Sea to Istanbul.

25

Istanbul

Istanbul was full of sounds that would never caress my ears, like the bells of the dead that rang at sunset daily. To compensate for my handicap, my keepers placed my body into one of the hollow tubes of the bells so that I would feel the vibrations of their exacting performance. My body was placed within the tube prior to their ringing so that I felt the whisper of the wind. My wrappings were removed and tiny wires were tied to my toes. These wires were then led outside the bells and attached to the wings of insects. The insects were exposed to the winds. The stronger the wind, the more agitated the insects became. Their wings vibrating in the wind vibrated the wire's vibratory sequence. I could feel the hush of the breeze that accompanied the morning. Also the soft hum of the bells sent shivers across my skin and deep into my bones. As the wind rose I felt the inner turbulence surge forth causing the muscles in my arms and legs to twitch and jerk.

By late afternoon the wind had become gusty flurries and with the coming of the night the squalls of a storm. When the storm reached a furious pitch, the bell ringers came. Even with the first clash of the bells, my body transcended itself. It was as if my very skin had grown ears. Every sound down to the slightest whisper was not heard, but sensed. It felt as if each quality of tone made itself known within each fiber of my body.

When I was removed from the tube, I felt sensations of awareness like I had never felt before. My body felt a new sense of consciousness, separated from the sense of sight, smell and sound. I still passed amongst strange hands that could give me no solace as to my fate, and my body vibrated under the storm with this new sense that touched my very bones.

26

Indian Ocean

The sticks had quieted and so had the voices of the children. I had lost count as to how many there were, but as my right eye peered over the water, I could see by the light of the moon that there were so many that they disappeared into the horizon beyond. They floated like corpses on the waters of the Indian Ocean. Their song was reduced to a soft whisper. My half-face had been placed upon a pedestal on the deck of a ship so that I would be closer to the stars. I was placed forward on the bow of the ship so that I would be closer to my destiny.

The calm of the Indian Ocean floated across my mind like a soothing balm. The stress and confusion of this journey had aged me. I did not know the fate of my body or the other side of my face. I may never be joined to them again. It may be that I am destined to remain forever as this lump of flesh with a consciousness of its own. Lost in my reverie, I failed to note a pale shadow, slowly edging itself along side of the ship.

"Only when the sands rise from this sea," spoke a voice that was soft and familiar. She floated there in the cold depths like a ghost. She seemed the same; the sadness in her eyes matched the deepness of the Indian Ocean. Her hair floated around her like reaching arms. "I'm sorry for you," she said. "It seems that you are the victim of some terrible joke. But did I not tell you? Only a profound madness can result from seeing me. Now you, like me, and all the unfortunate dead, wait for something to pull us from the black bile of our fate. Our impatience is unmeasured. We grope in the dark like children. We are afraid of the shadows, as they are shapeless forms that follow us in the night. Now you, like me, like all the passive bystanders, wander about like the blind Minotaur. Our sightless rage consumes us. Like the blind Minotaur, our maze is full of traps into which we ceaselessly blunder. Now you, like me, like all the drunken sailors, cry out in the night and there are no ears to hear. All of the poets who have bled to death have bled under this same vicious moon."

She screamed as if in agony and disappeared beneath the waves. I stared up at the moon that was full and blood red. The moon hung in silence, stared at me as if it knew some terrible secret. "When will it end?" I cried out. My only answer was silence and the memory of her words that echoed in my mind.

"Only when the sands rise from this sea."

27

Kobdo, Mongolia

Our entering the city of Kobdo brought cheers from its inhabitants. I was hoisted high with each rising roar. Louis and Ki walked, side by side, heading the procession. The rhythm of their walk was like the rise and fall of a heartbeat. The crowd's wailing cry matched the rhythmic pulse. I could see the rising towers of the ancient buildings; they seemed to heave a deep red hue. I watched the towers with rapt fascination, which turned into a shaking horror. The towers were covered with scorpions. The air was filled with an arachnid-like odor. I was brought before the temple whose appearance bled an evil that was stamped into its tall oaken doors.

The doors were adorned with carvings of scorpions and humans, all in varying degrees of transmutation. Their poses were obscene and grotesque. They crawled over each other, fondling the air and their sex. Their heads were thrown back in sensuous agony. They seemed to emerge from a forest of hands. The digital leaves tipped themselves in subliminal grace, touching the cheeks and groins of the dreadful reliefs. The massive doors slid open effortlessly, and I was escorted inside. My ear was immediately bathed in a sibilant intonation. The very walls seemed to hiss and whistle. Suddenly I felt a panic that flushed my cheeks like fire, and I struggled to see what was just beyond my sight.

Louis leaned over me with a malevolent smile. Ki with his mouth of crowds stood silently behind him. Nodding his head as if it were broken, Louis's foul breath assaulted my face when he spoke. "Welcome, to the temple of the scorpion. Your comfort so far has been carefully attended. The reasons shall be evident in the coming weeks. There are rituals that are to be performed in the temple that are unheard of beyond these walls. But I'm getting ahead of myself…" He turned to Ki and nodded, then turned back to me. "Some of those you shall have the opportunity to witness firsthand."

A shadow moved across the walls, a deep indescribable shadow that loomed across the room, filling it with its dread. I looked about, straining to see its source. A faint ticking noise ushered out from every corner. Louis and Ki moved out of my sight. The ticking became loader. The shadows moved. I looked past where Louis and Ki had been and there I saw the source of the shadow. A pall fell over me. I screamed.

28

Istanbul

Those new sensations that flooded my body like an avalanche of newly honed razors, razors that sliced across my nervous system in clear graceful strokes. Every pore of my skin seemed to itch. The hair follicles felt like they would explode, as if they were tiny volcanoes. I could now sense the time of day, the position of the sun, the features of someone's face, even the colors that surrounded me as if I had eyes. No, even more then if I had eyes, my senses could go to the very depth of things, to their hollow cores and into the crevices and folds of their very being.

A peasant by the name of Cistin presented me a plastic head. The resemblance to my own face was remarkable. The head had been part of a discarded store display. There were a few small cracks and a hole behind my left ear, but it was a good fit. It was placed upon my shoulders and for the first time in months I almost felt complete. Circumstances sometimes do not offer the freedom of choice in matters. I desired to enjoy the sites of Istanbul, to wander the streets and smell the scents that flowed from the foodstalls.

29

Madagascar

We dropped anchor just outside a small fishing village, in a small harbor. The air was hot and sticky, and flies hung in the sky like a huge buzzing blanket. There seemed to be something else in the ethers, something that held the air like an electrified current. This current clearly touched everyone, as I could see the hairs on their bare arms stand. Everyone was gathered on the deck, staring out in silence at a village that was as mute as a corpse. There was an overwhelming stillness that held everyone's gaze. The village stood alone; that aloneness was like a melancholic sigh.

From first glance, one would think the village extremely prosaic, as if it withstood the ravages of time, seeking sameness in itself that rested on the edge of the mundane, but as we stood staring at the empty village, something else occurred, something that was a displacement of the prosaic attitude of the village. From the depths of the shadows came a howl. The howl shuddered and released, shuddered and released, sending a chill through the air.

"Wolf," one of the sailors murmured. The howl answered an echoing mimic. It moved. Again the howl bit into the night and again it had moved. Either there was more than one or it moved with remarkable speed. From shadow to shadow the howl persisted. The ship's captain scuttled about the deck barking orders and pushing at his crew. Within minutes a small launch was lowered, and a handful of reluctant sailors and the right side of my face made for the shore. The rest of the crew gathered at the rail, watching in silence. It took some effort to convince the captain to allow my presence there, but after all that I'd been through, I felt that my presence was called for. There was something in the howl that lifted itself above the village rooftops that compelled me forward. The howl seemed as if it were exclusively for me. It came to me out of the dark, shattering the prosaic stillness. It rolled with the tide and rose in a beckoning call.

"Wolf," one of the rowers cried, trying to throw his oar aside and fling himself into the sea. The captain cuffed the sailor, barking insults and cursing the fates that brought him here. The howl answered his curse, freezing midword and visibly paling him with fear.

30

Kobdo Mongolia

My left eye twitched and glanced about frantically. A shadow manifested itself on the walls around me. My scream filled the hollow of the room. My left eye settled on a dark movement I could not quite identify. A giant scorpion sat upon an altar throne; its tail flicking in menacing movement. I looked to Louis and Ki accusingly. They mocked me with their smiles; their lips curved back like evil birds. What little light there was, undulated, casting shadows across their faces. Their features resembled masks, rubber doll-like masks, wolf-like masks, masks of ravens and of crocodiles. My field of vision clouded over as I felt the jaws of a trap enclose upon me. I began to dream.

Dream:

A large mouth sits on the horizon like an immense cavern, drawing me toward it with hypnotic osculation. The crowds of teeth are lingering photographs. Cracked and yellow, they stare like the expressionless dead. Their feet are tied together with white ribbon. Their voices are dull, a murmur in the dark.

1st Photograph: "Mankind has enjoyed its misery like an overcoat."

2nd Photograph: "The winter is long, and it is stained with the impossible. We wear the coats of the dead."

3rd Photograph: "The warring winds have called you. I see that you follow even though you are blind. I see that you come to pass through the dark hallways that are walled up within your skull."

4th Photograph: "Bricks and stones to cover your tomb. Silver will cover your eyes."

5th Photograph: "It is I who have stolen the shadows of birds. It is I who have nailed the shadows to the moon."

1st Photograph: "...And mankind has enjoyed its misery like an overcoat."

6th Photograph: "The mindless reality that flows from the bones of silence sits in the shadows waiting."

7th Photograph: "I am the luck of blackness; I am the swelling dark heart; I am murder, greed and corruption."

8th Photograph: "The mindless reality that is yours is like a river that is too deep to traverse."

9th Photograph: "There are no seasons such as this."

10th Photograph: "The pale moon of yesterday is weathered and torn. There are no sufficient yearnings that can equal the frayed memory clinging to my shirt tail."

1st Photograph: "...And mankind has enjoyed its misery like a overcoat. The lips are concealed in panic. They could be a woman's legs spreading to reveal a clitoral tongue. The crowds of ancient strangers gather as witnesses. Their morbid curiosity hangs in the balance."

11th Photograph: "I am the proud hag screaming the blues in a bag."

12th Photograph: "The night is swollen with purification. Dogs lay in the sand with their bellies opened. A chess game goes on within the cavity."

13th Photograph: "I am mangled in the thrashing machine of corn-belt America. I am luck stripped nude and flogged with chains."

14th Photograph: "Liar, liar...; nothing you have said even breathes of truth. Truth is lost in all that has been revealed."

1st Photograph: "...And mankind has enjoyed its misery like an overcoat."

31

Madagascar

The sand of the beach seemed as lonely as the village ahead. The howl gathered in the air like knotted rope, like a rope hungry for necks. The howl beckoned and waited. The shadows of the village lengthened towards us as if they were hands. Bony fingers pushed by the moon. Our feet left prints upon the beach; those sunken paths called for our return. The sand of the beach seems as lonely as the village ahead.

32

Varna, Bulgaria

A plastic head was placed upon the shoulders of my body. The head resembled a bird's head, with mechanical movements that jerked and twitched as if all the parts were not oiled, and the rusty gears struggled against each other. Nothing seemed quite right; nothing moved quite as it should. It seemed to flicker like an old movie. Every grimace was caught in freeze motion. Every twitch of my eye seemed to take a thousand years. I had a human body with a puppet head. I was a puppet master with no gloves or strings. I still had to travel enclosed and hidden so as not to arouse suspicion. I was surrounded by heavily armed bodyguards. They never smile except in death. There was an envelope in my pocket; it weighed heavy like a stone. It had become clear that it held an importance that I was not yet aware of. "You will have the opportunity for its use," a voice out of distant memory cries out.

33

Kobdo, Mongolia

My curse was not expressed in words, but in the unreality of my decapitation. I was caught in a continuous nightmare that wound itself like a fine tapestry. Somewhere at the back of my mind, I hear a howl. It shivered somewhere in another corner of my consciousness. Somewhere the moon was full. Somewhere the moon spoke of blood and tears. Somewhere a wolf howled for the hunt.

Dream:

On the shore of a deserted beach, a calm wind blows grains of sand. The shifting grains reveal and conceal the faces of drowned sailors. Their eyes speak of torments, of empty lonely hearts and of the storms that wash over their souls. I see three shapes on the beach's horizon. They are approaching. As they come closer, I can see they are nuns with their heads bowed in prayer. When they come up near me on the beach, they raise their heads simultaneously, looking me in the eye. I am shaken, for they each have a heavy growth of beard stubble on their faces. They are really men dressed as nuns. They wink and pass on by. I look out to the sea, which churns madly in a storm. In the far distance I see a woman in a small boat, its sails tattered and torn. She waves her arms as if she were in distress. I want to reach out and pluck her from the angry sea, but some invisible force holds onto me like a vise. I call out to her and my voice is carried away by the wind. She slumps down in the boat, holding her head in her hands weeping. Then she is swallowed up by the hungry mouth of the waves and was gone.

34

Madagascar

The sailor who carried the right side of my face was white with fear. He trembled and muttered to himself. The howl greeted us as we entered the village, but it was not a welcome of honor, but one of dread. The captain ran his thick fingers through his hair. "It seems that we walk into a village of the dead," he said. "There is nothing alive but that hellish howl. Even the air reeks of death. Whatever is here wants and waits, toying with us as if we were mice." He pulled a revolver from his waist and flipped off the safety catch. The click of the revolver was met with silence. It was an ear splitting silence that lay heavy in the air. The silence was broken by a scream. The scream shuddered on the edge of a light breeze, and then fell to nothing. "Where is Cakahan?" cried the captain, his voice rising in squeaky panic. "Where the hell is Cakahan? Cakahan! Cakahan! This is not a time for your fool jokes!"

We found a trail of blood that led to a small shack. We entered with a slow caution. The captain leveled his revolver in front of him with a shaky hand and took the lead. The walls were smeared with a thick darkness. The electric lamp cut through the darkness like a razor revealing the form of the sailor Cakahan. He hung from the wall a skinless hunk of meat. His eyes stared out into the emptiness. An incomprehensible babble fell from his lips. His eyes betrayed wildness and fell directly upon me. He shuddered slightly and spoke with words that hung in the room for what seemed like forever. "She-wolf." As he gasped his last breath, a howl pierced the darkness, a haunting howl that was both repulsive and frightfully inviting.

"Back to the ship!" the captain cried out. "Hurry, everyone, there is no time to waste! Back to the ship!"

"Wait," I pleaded. "There is something here. He said she-wolf, and I was told of a she-wolf that guarded a pass through the Kun Lun Mountains. She was not there, she is here. I need to know why."

"Why?" he stammered. "Why? I don't really give a damn, monsieur. A whole village is gone, dead perhaps. A member of my crew is hung here, stripped of his flesh. There is death in the darkness here and I want no part of it."

"But she may be the key to the whereabouts of the rest of my body. I must know. I cannot go about like this for the rest of my life."

Another howl penetrated the night. The captain spoke with a deep conviction, "I was hired to transport you to Cape Town and to protect you on the way. I speak frankly to you; of you I have fear. You are unnatural, a partial mask of a man. How you came to be or what will become of you, I do not care. I fear you, but I fear whatever hides in the darkness more. I will leave you here if you wish or take you to Cape Town, but either way, my ship leaves this damned harbor now."

35

Varna, Bulgaria

I crossed the room that was filled with sheep heads. They stared out with empty glass-eyes, glass like mine. Like mine, they possess an empty detachment. Like mine, they are tunnels of hollow caves, casting no shadows. But unlike mine they are without any psychic residue, for mine possess a certain dementia reserved only for the living.

So in this body that breathed such a dark mood, I stared out of plastic eyes at a world that I could not possess. I felt heaviness in my chest that weighed me down. My heart strained at a desire to understand, but the fog of vague notions stood at my shoulder like a stranger. I reached into my pocket and pulled out an envelope. It weighed heavily in my hand, like something dead, but I think it weighed heavily on my mind, because it was a dark question mark, with an edge sharper than a razor. I think that razor has slit my throat. The blood of my understanding flowed in an unceasing gush from the wound. I was a caged animal. I paced the floor from wall to wall, a beast caught up in the choking strands of a garrote. Reality had left me stranded. It was an inhuman farce. I felt I was a marionette, a shadow that had drowned in the swirling whirlpool of uncertainty. A scream was caught in my throat, because it was allowed to go no further beyond the plastic boundaries of my false head. This wetness that touched my cheek was so strange. My tongue desired to taste the salt of this warm, frail river, but all it can find was cold polyethylene.

36

Kobdo, Mongolia

Louis paced in front of me, his impatience mounting with each pass. The usual pallor of his face was deepening into the red of his rage. It gave me great pleasure to see that my silence caused him such agitation. The redness of his eyes was flames burning holes in the air. His breath was a hiss, scorning the walls. When my silence had reached the unbearable peak of his nerves, he turned to me and bared his teeth.

Ki, on the other hand, manifested the calm of stone. He sat with his legs crossed in silent meditation, smiling his smile of crowds. His mouth was full of vagrants, their backs all turned toward me. On their shoulders sat crows. Ki's presence was infinitely more disturbing than Louis. His cold, grey eyes held a depth of evil knowledge that was more ancient than that of Louis. His cold stare penetrated me to the very depths, like ice, like a glacial knife. There was more dread in that stare than all the horrible threats that Louis could muster. Ki's eyes held an unknowable darkness that betrayed nothing. I'd never known such impenetrable depth, such horrible intense maldolorian evil. Ki held the hearts of crows gripped in the stony stillness of the sea. His grey eyes of steel were those of a harpy. The strangers in his mouth were clouded with remorse.

Louis brought himself before my face. "You are a fool," he said. "I am tired of your trying my patience. The time of toying with you is through. The game that is played around fear is getting boring, and death is a long time. Now where is the location of your body?" I looked at him with puzzlement. "Please don't act the part of the innocent. You must know that there hangs a psychic thread connecting the parts. It is foolish to hide the truth from me. I am more powerful than you, by a thousand years. I could crush your will with my will, but I prefer politeness."

In the panic of my situation I had not thought that there was any link to the location of my missing body parts. But of course! I could feel certain waves of heat. I could feel nerve endings. If indeed there were knowledge of the location of my missing pieces, then I must protect them at all cost. Louis bent over me, and his hot breath caressed my

169

face. The heat of it burned me. "Now tell me where it is!" he demanded. I stared at him in silence.

37

Varna, Bulgaria

An officer of the police stood in the doorway. He clicked his heels with a smart abruptness. "Lieutenant Charkas at your service, sir," he snapped, saluting as if the act were forced and contrived. "I am to escort you to the border, where further instructions will be waiting. Come please, a car is running outside and there is no time to waste.

I quickly gathered my things and followed him down to the street. The street was filled with a thick acrid smoke. It was a smoke filled with displeasure, violence and hunger. It was a smoke of discarded hats. Desire clung to the air like a fist. The waiting car was a long black Mariah; so long it appeared to be a snake. Lieutenant Charkas hurried me into the back seat and bade the driver to go. As we turned onto the main drive, we were met by throngs of angry people. Their fists were clenched, their teeth clutched tightly and their eyes burned with rage. They pounded their fists on the windows as we passed. Their shouts in Bulgarian escaped my understanding, but the guns they pulled from beneath their coats made clear their intent. Rage trampled across the windows. Daylight was smothered by the smoke.

Charkas turned to me, his face was pale and taut. He looked like a man who had not slept in days or one who was experiencing the tremors of madness. "I am sorry my friend," he sighed, "but my country is torn with bitterness and revolution. Times such as these are confused, and people draw parallels and conclusions that have nothing to do with the situation. They see your arrival at this inopportune time as a significant symbol of their situation."

"What is their situation, Lieutenant?" I asked, unable to tear my gaze away from the angry mob.

"Well, they have been exposed to a massive chemical spill and their bodies are disintegrating at a rapid pace. The government has put a false face forward and denied any existence of the situation."

I turned to Charkas, who was frowning with great displeasure. "So what has that to do with me?" I asked.

"Well," he replied, "you, too, are in possession of a false face."

38

At Sea

The winds were becoming cooler as we approached Cape Town. The crew (what is left of it) were shaken with fear. It had followed us. It was on board the ship somewhere. Despite the efforts to locate it, it eluded us like a mist. The blood-shuddering howl haunted the night. Blood marked its passing. Those of the crew who were unable to cope with this flesh-rending reality had succumbed to a stuttering madness. They either stared blindly out to sea or had given themselves over to the inky depths of a watery grave.

39

Kobdo, Mongolia

Ki, who sat in silence, turned to Louis and gave him a simple nod. Louis rose to his feet, turned, and left the room. I was alone in the room with Ki. I had never felt fear so deeply or despaired so fully. Ki's eyes, like hot coals, burned deep into the back of my mind. His smile was dry and bitter. He placed foul-smelling incense into a bowl and began to mutter. The tone of his voice was like bells, but bells muted in blood. My mind began to wrench as if pulled by storms. Torn and maimed, it screamed in silence and a vapor descended upon it. How long I lingered in an empty vapor, I didn't know, but as it lifted I heard Ki speaking. "You may enter now, Louis. I have obtained the answers we seek."

40

At Sea

The crew had all but abandoned the ship. There were only a few skeletons that remained and those seemed to be mindless ghosts that drifted across the deck. They performed their duties in complete defeat and with unseeing eyes. I believed them to be possessed by an unholy presence that haunted this ship. The night was still filled with howls. The first mate was found that morning hanging upside down in an obscene pose, like a mockery of the crucifixion. He was opened up from his groin to his chest; all of his organs had been removed and placed neatly in a circle around him. Inside the cavity was placed a candle and a photograph. It appeared to be an altar, an altar of death and disease. I had the captain move me closer to this obscene altar so that I might have a closer look at the photo. The photo was of me. If I had a stomach I would have vomited, but all I could do was choke on the tears that fell from a single eye.

41

Kobdo, Mongolia

Louis stood above me, the hot coals of his eyes burning deeply within my split soul. "You see," he said. "It was quite easy, and you felt only a little pain. It is time to gather together the trinity and dissolve the barriers that have confounded us. You have hoped for a savior and have found none. You will find no saviors here, but only the prestigious collectors of flesh. Death rests on my lips, and I love the taste of blood." He turned, ushering all the attendants out of the room. "We now have possession of your other face, and time will bring us the body."

A deep sense of foreboding fell across me. Now, surely all was lost. All perception of salvation was lost. I believed myself truly hell-bound. I quivered at the thought of what my delicious passions had brought upon me. All of my will had been stretched to the breaking point. The thin thread of bonding that connected my parts had betrayed me and now I was to be forsaken as lost.

42

Romania

We had just passed over the Danube into Romania. Charkas has bid me luck and farewell. I felt that what was left of me was in grave peril. I had been taken by a group of gypsies who were headed north. Many of the tribe crossed themselves and touched their foreheads with thumb and index finger displayed as a crucifix. There were no smiles here, only a faint muttering amongst themselves.

"You must forgive them their fears," a voice from behind me spoke. I turned and saw with my glass eyes a bulky man with a full beard. His hair was long and tangled around his shoulders. "My name is Ashba," he continued. "I am the leader of this group. Fear is a constant thing here in these times. Romania is an old place filled with dark superstitions. My people know what it is that you flee, and they fear it will find you while you are with them."

"And you?" I asked. "Are you afraid?"

"I am an educated man," he replied, "but even so, I cannot discount the old beliefs. Within myth lies the grains of truth and for that I am afraid. You have opened a doorway into hell and from that opening evil rises like a foul smoke. Only you and that envelope which has been guarded so carefully will decide the course of destiny."

43

Off the Coast of Cape Town

Cape Town was a haunted graveyard. The captain's radio calls to the shore were met with a shroud-like silence. The dead had no voice and Cape Town had fallen victim to a deathly silence. It was only the captain and I who were left, floating on the sea like jetsam. The port we sought for safe refuge was now a threatening corpse that we had to leave behind. I asked the captain what we should do, but he just stared off into the empty blackness of the sea. The only answer we could obtain from Cape Town was the blood-curdling howl that sifted through the darkness. The captain's face was pale as death; his eyes darted back and forth in his head like bees. "We must leave this place," he muttered, staring at the shore. "This is a dangerous and foul place to be." I nodded my head in agreement, for this was a very dangerous place, but I feared that I had run out of safety nets and that the evil was closing in on me. This unholy presence that haunted the ship had eluded us. Every inch had been searched and overturned, but nothing was there but the rats, and even they hurried to abandon the ship.

"Captain," I shuddered, "perhaps we should abandon the ship. It seems hopeless to stay here. If we do then we may end up as the others."

44

Adrift at Sea

We had left Cape Town behind, following the shoreline looking for a safe harbor. The insistent howl followed along the shoreline, reminding us of its presence. The captain himself was starting to slip into madness. He babbled insistently. The babble ranged from the nonsensical to the absurd, aspersed with lurid limericks and ghastly nursery rhymes.

45

Kobdo Mongolia

Ki had rejoined Louis and whispered into his ear. He glanced in my direction and winked a knowing eye. He grinned; his teeth full of crowds were all laughing. Louis turned and whispered in turn, into my ear, "Well, the hounds have found the rabbit. Does that not give you pause? There is nothing for you now but to accept your fate and taste the bitter wine of defeat." I shuddered at the thought. Louis's breath stank of stale blood and the rotting flesh of the dead. "It's the days of wine and roses. The wine is spoiled and the roses have wilted, its petals fallen to dust. We now have possession of your head, now we have the brain. Where the brain goes, the body follows." I convulsed as Louis and Ki laughed a dark humor that only they knew.

46

Adrift at Sea

I awoke, my body covered with sea mist. My glass eyes darted about looking for the captain. I saw his lifeless corpse staring blindly out to sea. A look of absolute terror was frozen upon his face. The gulls had already arrived for the feast. One of the gulls landed on the captain's head, bent over and neatly plucked out one of his eyes. It tilted its head back and swallowed. Turning its head towards me, the gull spoke with a rasping voice, "Caught in a dilemma, aren't you?" The gull hopped down onto the plank directly across from me. "I wager that your situation is about to get worse, in fact dinner is about to be served in the banquet room of the doomed, and the main coarse is you!" I looked to the horizon and approaching fast was a shadow ship sailing under full sail. Its sails of spider webs and fog billowed in the wind. In moments it would be upon me, and I would be lost. I felt as if I were spinning dizzily out of control. If I could have vomited, I would have released the bile of centuries. The fog seemed to overtake me, and I felt darkness cover me like a shroud.

47

Aboard the Black Tooth

When I regained my senses, I was surrounded by a pack of wolf-like creatures. They stood like men, but the sharpened teeth betrayed the guise. They chatted amongst themselves, prodding me with sticks and hurling insults at me. Their chatter suddenly ceased and they parted, making room for a tall, dark figure that seemed to float down the pathway made by the crew. He stood all of eight feet, a wisp of a man, more shadow than flesh and blood. His eyes were crimson and as deep as empty space. They turned their heads so as to not look into those flaming eyes.

He stood above me and ran one of his long fingernails across his cheek leaving a trail of blood on his pale flesh. He bent over me and spoke with a voice as thin as his skin. "You know that I am being paid well to deliver you, but I am an impatient man: Try my patience and I will see you at the bottom of this ocean, good pay or not. But to ensure your cooperation, I have arranged a suitable place for you to spend this voyage." He then produced a small lead coffen. He picked me up and placed me inside. Before shutting the lid, he snarled down at me, "Sleep tight."

48

Romania

A sense of panic had set in. I feared all was lost. I had heard nothing. My face seemed to be but a memory. I had forgotten my own features. The gypsies spoke in whispers, carefully guarding their discussions. I could only faintly feel the vibrations of their words as they blanketed up my body. Perhaps I had died and this was the afterlife. Perhaps I had never lived at all, except that I was but a fragment of someone else's lurid dream. I was being prepared for some journey, but its destination was cloaked in secrecy and shadow. I wanted to cry out to someone, but the room felt empty now. I was abandoned to my loneliness and despair. My future seemed cloaked in darkness. I was a ship with no sail to catch the wind and no rudder to guide my way. I was floundering in a dream that had no end.

49

Kobdo Mongolia

The light was blinding as my eye opened to a highly decorated room. As my eye became accustomed to the light, my gaze fell upon a familiar object across the room: it was the other side of my face. I was almost jubilant at the sight. My excitement was cut short. I was being lifted from the box that contained me and I was being laid gently upon a piece of red silk. Two figures stood above me, their stares and demeanor did nothing to dampen my anxiety over the situation. One of the figures grinned, and his mouth was full of strangers. "Welcome," he intoned like a funeral bell. "Welcome to my palace of pain. My name is Ki, and my friend here and I are delighted to have you join us. I think you recognize your other half across the room." His crooked fingers pointed at my other face lying on a small table. The look of sheer panic was in its one eye. "The return of the rest of you is now being arranged. Those you thought you trusted have seen the error of their loyalties and will soon, in exchange for their own lives relinquish their prize treasure." Ki opened his mouth to a toothy grin of crowds. The photographs that were his teeth had began to laugh, a hysterical, maniacal laughter that drooled menace and madness.

50

On the Road

I felt the rattle of the road, deep within my bones. We were traveling northeast, by my guess, on a road of blind destination. I could feel the laughter and whispers of the gypsy troop that carried my carefully wrapped body across unknown lands toward an unknown future. Optimism has long ago abandoned me to a fate of uncertainty and doom. Night was falling; I could feel the drop in the night mist, moistening the blanket in which I was wrapped. When darkness had descended, and all the gypsies had fallen asleep, a lone, faceless figure knelt beside my wrapped body and whispered. "In a few days it will all be over, your despair; your panic, your uncertainty and your madness. I will be fabulously wealthy and you will be dead." I wanted to scream out but with no mouth to form my words, I just lay there as a motionless mummy entombed in linen shrouds. "Your journey is nearly over; Hell will greet you with open arms. I am truly sorry, but the scent of wealth was too strong and I had to make the choice between my life or your death: the choice is very clear. I will weep for you and collect my tears and give them as an offering to the gods for forgiveness of my treachery."

51

Kobdo Mongolia

Louis stood between the two sides of my face. He gleefully nodded to each. "Time has a way of adjusting the fate of a situation, doesn't it? One day you are whole, a man of intelligence and strength, of sound body and mind, and the next, you're a blithering madman lost in the nightmare of your life. It's a comedy of errors filled with such dramas that only the mad can think up. It's the wickedness of a dark mirth that consumes the mind and leaves it stranded in distant lands or in strange locked rooms. You are bound by a straightjacket of your own making.

You are shattered into a thousand pieces, and I am here to gather all the pieces and reassemble them like a crazy jigsaw puzzle. What you once were has slipped away, and what you will become will be determined by your own dreams, dreams that have led you here like a bull to the slaughter."

Ki entered the room and whispered into Louis's ear. I could hear the crowds in Ki's mouth, whispering and laughing. Ki nodded his head in my direction, his grin producing a mouthful of grins. Simultaneous screams issued from both sides of my face as trumpets blared. The huge scorpion-doors swung open and six pallbearers carried in a stretcher with a convulsing bundle wrapped in linen shrouds. The convulsing bundle was set on the floor. The pallbearers quickly left the room except for one. The remaining bearer bowed his head and spoke with a trembling voice, "I have done as you requested, Master. Please, my reward, and let me be gone from this foul place. Louis glanced at Ki and then back to the trembling man.

"Of course, your reward," Louis spitted out. "We mustn't forget the man's reward. Is that not true, Ki?"

Ki nodded and grinned. Ki open his mouth wide, his teeth a seething mass of nightmares. The nightmares reached out and pulled the poor man into the gapping mouth where it closed upon him like a steel trap. A small amount of bloody drool fell from Ki's lips. Louis handed Ki a napkin remarking, "Manners, Ki, manners." Ki wiped his mouth and grinned with bloody lips. Louis bent and began to unwrap the bundle on the floor. On the floor my body convulsed, on the tables my split faces screamed. I could hear clicking sounds approaching. Louis raised his head. "At last, the stage is set for a banquet of murders and thieves. The depraved will gather in these halls to feast on your memories. All that you have loved will be devoured; all that you were will be consumed. Your tears will moisten their palates and your breath will become smoke dissipating in the wind." Louis raised his hands; Ki bowed low and moved back against the wall. The clicking noise became louder as the doors slowly swung open. "Come, my children, come and partake of one man's wickedness, nourish yourself on the bile of his life, satiate yourselves upon his consciousness. It is no longer his, but yours to drink like a fine wine. Three courses of a man who could not wake up, for he is consumed by his dreams and they are you." The doors opened fully and my eyes fell upon a parade of scorpions, clicking with anticipation. My body convulsed uncontrollably, and both sides of my face screamed simultaneously. Screamed and screamed.

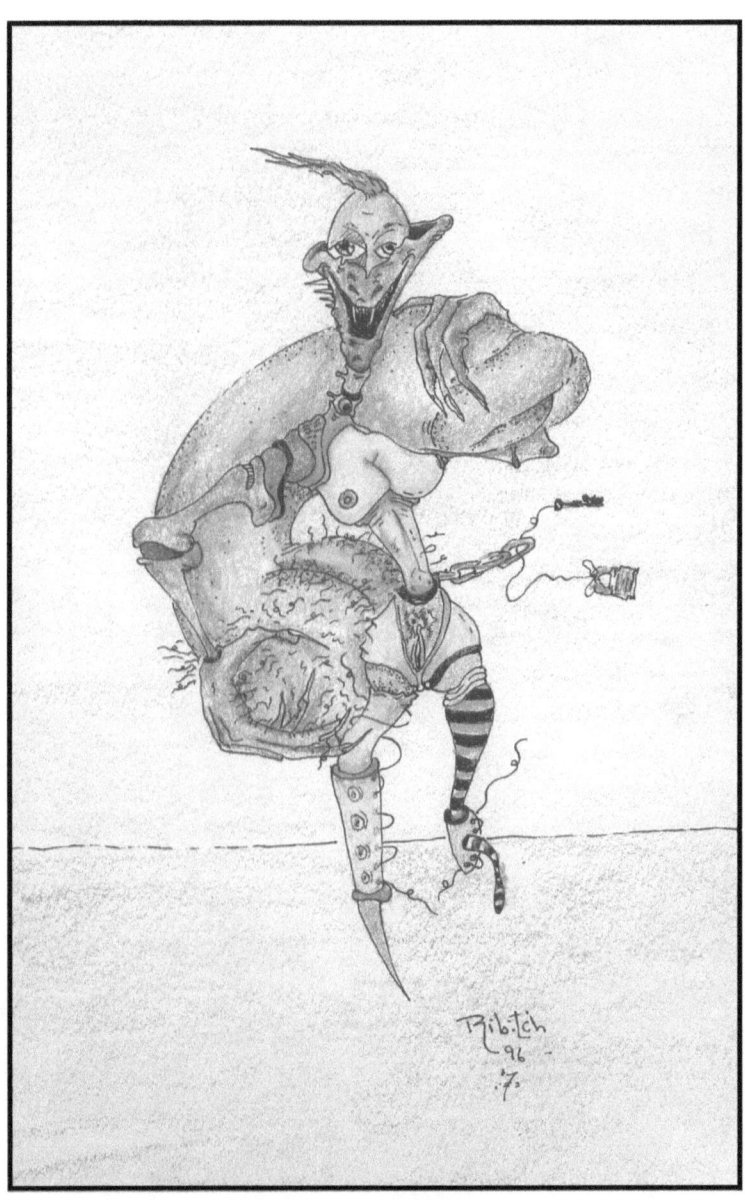

www.ingramcontent.com/pod-product-compliance
Lightning Source LLC
Chambersburg PA
CBHW052132170626
46812CB00004B/1371